Dragon

(If You Couldn't Tell)

Dragon

(If You Couldn't Tell)

By Brynne Nelson

Illustrated by Randilee Warner

for Mom and Dad

Who listened to it

All those years ago

And who have supported me

Through this whole crazy process

Acknowledgements

I wrote the first draft of *Dragon (If You Couldn't Tell)* ten years ago (ish,) so there is a lot of thanking to do.

First, I have to thank my parents. I know I did that in the dedication, but this book never would have even been finished if they hadn't urged me to keep writing, keep working, keep reading it aloud to them in the evenings during my junior year of high school.

In the intervening ten years, I got married and had three kids (I did other things, too.) Thanks have to go to my husband, who puts up with me getting out of bed at midnight to "go write something down real quick" for an hour, and to my children—currently all under age five—who really only understand that "Mommy made this book" and that Daddy reads to them at bedtime. They behave very well (mostly) when I am trying to get writing done.

I have to thank my beta readers. My Grandma, Elaine Bonham, gave me notes after two days with the manuscript. My friends in The Writing Gals and Fantasy Writers Forever! on Facebook, who encouraged me through the horrible editing process, are rock stars. And I can't forget my youngest beta reader, Tilly, age 8, whose enthusiasm really made the difference between finishing the book and giving up. There's also my writing partner-in-crime, my cousin Jane, who lets me pick her brain every day or so, and my ever-supportive oldest brother McKay who does the same.

My artist, Randilee Warner, was patient with my constant anxiety-driven checkups and squeezed me into her crazy schedule. Additionally, she turned out art that I never could have managed myself, but seemed to have popped right out of my head.

The audiobook would never have gotten off the ground without my brother Keith and his keen ears and willingness to listen to endless snippets. And Dad came in here, too, of course, knowing things about audio that go way over my head. I also never would have recorded a single minute if not for my neighbor Sam Macias, who loaned me his audio equipment. Lastly, my thanks to Karlee Porter for watching my three kids while I recorded.

Of course, hats off to Dad (and Mom with him, naturally,) and Grandma, for investing not only time but money into getting this project "out there." If you're reading this, it's because of their investment.

I feel I should thank my late grandfather, Kay Moon, for passing on the writing bug in my genes. I'd never have put pen to paper if not for Grandaddy.

Always, always, I thank my God for any gifts or talents I possess, for the strength to keep going, and for the love that gives me purpose.

Thank you, lastly, to my readers. You are what makes this writing business fun past the first chapter. Your delight, your support, your contact, and your appreciation make it all worth it.

-Brynne Nelson, 2019

INTRODUCTION

There's nothing quite like saving the world to make one truly awesome. I should know, I did it. And while I've always been amazing in pretty much every way, it certainly didn't *hurt* my reputation. I know I sound braggy, but I just don't know what else to tell you. It's the truth. I'm incredible.

I suppose, if you're going to read my story, I should tell you more than just how wonderful I am. My name is Izznae— lovely to make my acquaintance, I'm sure. I've been told I'm a *gorgeous* female, although I suppose my opinion on that could be a little skewed. I was hatched and raised near a volcano on the northern edge of the main continent, Daiines. Right now, I'm blue, but I don't think it will last; blue's really not my color. If you want to recognize me, you might notice, instead of my color, the longer snout we volcano-dwellers often have and the scar on my—

I beg your pardon? What are you confused about? You… you didn't know I was a dragon? Excuse me, I'll be right back.

I'm sorry, I had to go laugh somewhere else, so I wouldn't accidentally light this paper on fire.

Oh, I see. You didn't think dragons could write, did you? Of all the prejudiced notions! Why would anyone assume that only humans had the ability to write? Do you know how brilliant and magical and *incredible* the average dragon is?

Never mind, I don't have time to deal with *your* personal problems. If you want me to care, write your own book.

Ahem.

What was I saying? Ah, yes, the scar on my right wing, near the snorkius.

How in Daiines could you not know what a snorkius is? Didn't you sing that song to learn body parts when you were little? You know, "head, knoppers, snorkius and jeed…" No? Ah, well. If you want to understand this story, you'll have to know more about dragons. I suppose this means a diagram. Hang on a minute.

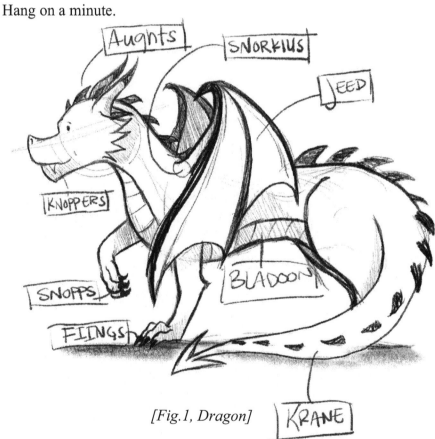

[Fig.1, Dragon]

Now, did that help? Yes, you can take a minute to appreciate how incredibly cool dragons are. You know, right now I almost wish we were friends so that you could revel in the reflected light of my grandeur. Unfortunately, I am not accepting offers of friendship at this time. But humans are cool too, I guess. I mean, you guys have…hair. And, um, lips? And livers—no dragon has a liver! And, in my experience, a fair amount of courage.

[Fig. 2, Human]

Oh, is that why you're reading this? To hear about my experience with human beings? Well, lucky you. That's what I'm writing about. Which, I guess, is why you picked up this book. Well, then, I don't want to keep you waiting. I'd best get on with the story.

CHAPTER ONE

So there we were, each trying hard to pretend the other didn't exist. If I could've left the cave right then and there, I would have. I know Dibbins felt the same way. But it was just too *shiny*, and besides, going outside would mean our deaths—the dwarves were right outside the door, keeping watch. But mostly it was the shine, the luster of the treasure, that kept me from trying to escape.

Oh, you want me to start at the *beginning*? Well aren't we just demanding today. "Tell me a story," "Overlook my prejudiced view of your species," "Make the story make sense!" But the beginning is so *boring*.

Fine.

I told you I'm a volcano dragon. And, no, before you ask, we don't actually live *in* the volcano. Magma can even melt dragon scales after a while. (We do eat the rocks the volcano spews out.) My volcano is a charming place called Spendidium, located in a lovely northern corner of my home continent. You're not welcome there.

What was that? No, of course I'm not the only dragon on Spendidium. Look, you call your house yours and your city yours. I call my volcano mine. Can I get on with my story?

Thank you.

So. I hatched near the volcano. My parents were thrilled when I burned my way through my egg in record-breaking time. My father gloated about it for weeks to everyone in our clan. So from my first days, all of the dragons nearby—who were mostly my absurdly large extended family—knew I was a champion fire-breather. They all thought it was a sign of my great, dragony deeds to come, and my parents and I basked in the glory of that for a while. Then, when the praise started to wind down, a problem arose: I realized that I didn't care. Not about breathing fire, that is (I do still enjoy praise.)

Well, think about it! I grew up near a *volcano*. Fire just doesn't excite me a whole lot.

Glitter, on the other hand…

Volcanoes are bright, hot places, yes. They are also places with lots of dull-looking (if delicious) gray and black rocks. Plants burn away fast if they grow at all. The dragons are the most exciting-looking part about a volcano, and considering our tradition of camouflaging ourselves with the scenery around us, we're not often that great to look at.

I saw you look back at my diagram. I understand that you're amazed by me and cannot possibly see how I might be bored by dragons. Newsflash: I *am* one. Do you like to just sit and look at other humans?

Oh, come on. I didn't mean like *that.* Attractiveness aside, you find your species boring. I can't really blame you, since your people are less fascinating than mine, but even so, I found my neighbors dull—just as you might.

My cousins were all hotheads who liked to play together near the volcano's core. They also liked to call me names like "freak" and "nut" and "pofedd" (that last one is *very* rude.) They even occasionally resorted to physically harming me when they knew I couldn't roast them for it because a parent was watching. Fortunately, though, there's more to life than socialization. I had discovered my true passion the first moment I left the egg, and I clung to it as I grew.

You see, dragon eggs *sparkle*. Nesting mothers cover their eggs in stuff from their hoards. I think it started out as protection—cover the shell in diamonds and nothing can hurt your baby. Then, when the draclet (baby dragon) hatches and burns away the shell, the mother takes her diamonds back. However, egg-decorating has become an art, and a competitive one. As my mother's first egg, I hatched from an award-winning, fully gilded, jewel-encrusted egg that hummed softly from enchanted treasure. The first moment I saw that mound of valuables, my eyes glittered.

Look, it's my story, and I'm going to tell it my way. So what if the sparkle in my eyes was a reflection of the jewels? I still knew I'd found my passion. Nothing in Daiines could ever be as beautiful, as moving, as that pile of shinies.

I sometimes couldn't talk, couldn't *think*, about anything but hoarding and gold and jewels and sparkles.

The other kids (why young goats and young dragons have the same name, I'll never know) thought my obsession was weird, which is why they picked on me. Actually, my parents worried about it too—I'd heard them discuss it when they thought I was asleep. They thought I liked treasure more than was healthy for any dragon. Which, considering that we're known around the whole world for our hoarding, is saying something.

They just…they didn't *understand!*

Yeah… unfortunately for everyone, dragons have teenage years too.

Actually, that's sort of where the story *you* care about starts. Blah blah I was a social outcast, blah blah the other kids would've picked on me except that I (being a champion fire-breather) would've burned their tails off, blah blah uncomfortable with the society on Spendidium.

The story picks up when I was nine hundred and seventy-two. Approximately thirteen in human years, as far as development goes. I'd just gotten home after being chased out of the magma pool by some idiots who thought it would be funny to try and dump lava into my eyes.

My mother and I were fighting.

Not like *fighting* fighting. Even among dragons, clawing or biting or burning your mother will get you SENT TO YOUR ROOM by your father. Or rather, SENT TO YOUR CAVE. Whatever. Anyway, my mother and I were fighting because I wanted to go off to build my hoard, something dragons usually do in their thousand-three-hundreds.

My mother put her foot down.

"Young lady, go to your cave! You will stay there until you learn to control your temper!"

"But Mother, I'm old enough to take care of myself!" I protested. "It's not like I need you to feed or clothe me, I'm not some *mammal—*" I'd gone too far; where my mother had been flaming with rage a moment before, now she was ice-calm and hurt.

"That's technically true," she said at last. "But that kind of needs aside, you are still a child, and I am still your mother. Besides, we follow laws of tradition around here. It's part of being a dragon."

"I thought no one could tell dragons what to do," I grumbled.

"No one but the gods and other dragons, Izznae. Parents are supposed to take the lead in every family, including among dragons.

"Plus, if you move out, your sister will never forgive you," she added, trying not to smile at the victory she knew she'd just scored.

Mooninga. My eight hundred and thirty-year-old sister. Most of the time she was my best friend—my only friend. Some of the time she was what my mother used against me to get her way. For now, at least, I knew I'd lost the battle.

Roaring my frustration loudly enough that all the dragons in Spendidium probably heard me, I flew out of our cave.

Stupid tradition. Stupid *rules*. I landed in a cavern across the volcano from mine, a place I liked to go just to be alone. It wasn't big enough to be a home cave for even one dragon, but it was nice enough just to sit in. The walls were made of some reflective kind of igneous rock, and I could sit back, close my eyes, and listen to the waves of lava as they lapped against the stone.

What? It's soothing.

I settled down to do just that. But instead of the gentle roar of flaming molten rock slowly burning through the mountain, I heard an odd scraping sound.

Urggh, rghkk. Crrchh. Eeeggh.

Definitely scraping sounds.

Curious, I looked around for a source.

Little puffs of dust materialized, wafting upward from the floor in the back of the cave. That was a little freaky, even for me. I lumbered over to the little dirt-spout, smashing my jeeds (that's wings, remember?) as close to my body as I could. (I told you, the cave's not big.) I took a cautious sniff. Dust clouded my nostrils, and I sneezed, spouting fire.

"Ouch!" Came a muffled voice from below me. (Actually, because there was nearly-solid rock between us, what I heard was more like, "rffch!") I leaned forward to investigate, and the stone underneath me started to crumble. I jumped back just in time; what had been the floor was suddenly the top of an almost-vertical tunnel. There were some odd clattering and banging sounds, then silence. I edged forward and looked down into the hole.

A very dirty human looked up at me.

He stared at me for a moment, a mix of surprise and horror on his face. Then he—as far as I knew, anyway, it was male—took a breath, choked a little on the still-dusty air, and looked up at me boldly.

"Help me up," he said. I just looked at him.

"Are you telling me what to do, little meatball?" I asked.

"Yes, I am. Help me up." I was so startled that I wriggled my rokk—my "arm"—into the pit and grabbed him with my snopps. Then, walking backward, I dumped both of us on the floor of the cave nearer the opening, where there was space to sit.

"It's *hot* in here," the human whined. I rolled my eyes.

"Little meatball, you climbed into a volcano—or, nearly in. What exactly were you expecting?" The human was pouring sweat—probably from the heat and from the shock of my awesomeness—which cleaned the dirt off him in little stripes.

Ugh. Good thing dragons don't sweat. Or get dirty, actually. Our scales, being magical, reject dust, dirt, and any other filth.

"But seriously, why are you here?" I asked impatiently.

"I..um...well..." he trailed off with a string of noncommittal words and awkward stammers. I continued to glare at him while I considered.

Humans. Most of what I knew of them came from old legends. Dragons who *didn't* live by volcanoes were more likely to interact with the little two-legs, and even for *them* it was rare. I'd heard that the princesses could be useful, but this dirty fellow was not a princess. There were also tales that the knights could be pesky. I didn't think this was a knight; at any rate, he hadn't pulled a sword out yet. I'd also heard that some of them were very fond of treasure.

Ohhhh no.

"You're after treasure, aren't you?" I demanded.

"What?"

"You can't have it. I'll burn you to a crisp first."

Okay, I wouldn't have burned him to a crisp. I prefer my meat medium-well done, if I have to eat meat at all; I'd much rather have a nice crunchy piece of basalt with a light sandstone on the side. Anyway, the message got across; his eyes got all wide and scared-looking. It was funny.

"I'm not that stupid." He said.

"Um. You broke into a dragon's cave. I'd say you're pretty stupid."

"*No*," he said, a little too loudly. "No. I mean, yes, I broke into a dragon's cave—"

"'No, no, yes'?" I asked. "You're not making any sense." I grinned at him, showing my silver knoppers. "I suggest you start making sense."

He swallowed forcibly but showed no other outward signs of fear. If humans could possibly ever impress me, that would have been impressive. You know, *if*. He breathed in slowly, looking down, then raised his head again and stared straight into my eyes.

"I didn't come to steal your treasure, dragon. I came for help stealing someone else's."

CHAPTER TWO

Teenagers do some really stupid things, even when they're dragons. Sometimes they vandalize the home cave of the Eeggan, the peace-keeping dragon. Sometimes they pull dangerous stunts to get the attention of dragons that they think are cute. Sometimes they stay way too long at the magma pool with their friends instead of coming home by curfew. And sometimes they decide that they're tired of being treated like kids and fly away to steal treasure from evil dwarves with a human on their back.

Oh, yeah. About that.

After the human made his little pronouncement about stealing treasure, it took me a second to regain my composure (and don't pretend it didn't surprise you too!) First of all, since when did humans ask dragons for help? As far as I knew, dragons (especially volcano dragons) and humans didn't mix.

Like, ever. Remember how you didn't even know we existed until I told you? Point proved.

Beyond that, here was a human openly admitting that he wanted to rob somebody. As I understood it, humans just didn't do that. They lied, they cheated, they backstabbed. They had invented a whole special kind of dishonesty called "politics," which gave me a headache when we studied it in our "Creatures of Daiines" class. Humans were not known for being forthright—in fact, they were known far and wide for the opposite. All in all, I was not ready for this grimy little snack to inform me that he was going to go hijack some treasure and I was going to help him.

I figured that it must've taken so much courage that it kinda made me want to let him hang around.

So I settled against the wall of the cave more comfortably and eyed him.

"I can't keep calling you meatball." I said. "It's making me hungry. I am the great dragonness Izznae. Who are you?"

"*Izznae*," he said, turning my name over in his mouth. "Can I call you *Iz*?"

I frowned. This human kept surprising me. Dragons don't have nicknames. I love when people make mistakes like that, it makes them so mockable.

"Can I call you Dibbins?" I asked, pulling the sounds for the silly name out randomly. He looked at me for a long moment.

"Dibbins. Alright. It's a deal."

I had not planned on that. Somehow this bite-size person had managed to give me a nickname, possibly the first in dragon history. On the plus side, though, I could now refer to him as "Dibbins," an embarrassing name if there ever was one.

"I can live with that, I guess." I told him. "Now, explain about this treasure heist of yours."

So he did. Apparently, there was a clan of evil dwarves living under one of the mountains nearby, in a place called Coortain. They had a huge amount of stuff that they'd made or collected over the years, most of it very, *very* valuable. Dibbins wanted to break into the mountain and make off with as much of the lode as he could. There were two problems, though. First, the dwarves were all fully capable of killing Dibbins if he was caught (which was likely,) and, second, he had no way of hauling all the treasure away if he managed to get to it. Which is why he wanted a dragon's help. He figured that even if the dwarves could easily chop him to bits, they wouldn't dare take on a dragon. Plus, I could carry much more treasure than he could. And, he supposed, a dragon would be in support of treasure-gathering. Then, after we had pulled off the greatest bit of thievery in a hundred years (if you're wondering, the one before us was the robbery of my uncle Nathteschew) we would split the treasure in half and each go home rich.

"So… what do you think?" Dibbins asked me tentatively.

"And I'd get half the treasure?" I asked again.

"If you're up for it."

I considered. On the one snop (I believe humans say, "on the one hand"), I would get to start my hoard off very nicely. I would be going on an adventure that no one in my family could compete with, and I'd get to prove that I was old enough to handle my own life. Plus I'd be wiping out evil in the form of any dwarves I might toast, and keeping the humans happy so they wouldn't decide to go dragon-hunting or something. On the other snop...

Nope. Nothing. This was the most awesome idea I'd ever heard.

"You know… I sort of like it." I said, trying and failing to sound nonchalant. Dibbins grinned.

"Well, when can we leave?" He asked.

"Just let me leave a note for my parents—" Dibbins snorted in disbelief or amusement. I glowered, and he looked apologetic. "—and we can be on our way." I said.

"You don't have to pack anything?" He asked.

"Like what," I asked, "clothes? I'm a dragon. We don't wear clothes. Food? I eat rocks. *Dragon.* And rocks are not exactly hard to find in the mountains. I might see if there are some extra *brains* lying around for you to use, though." Dibbins sighed.

"Excuse my concern, Iz. Let's get going."

So I scratched out a note for my mother, telling her that I loved her, was going on an adventure, and would be back soon, and then Dibbins climbed onto my back.

"Ow." I said. He was sitting on my snorkius.

"Sorry," he said, sliding off. "Where should I sit?"

"*Behind* my jeeds, between these two aughts," I told

him, changing the aughts in question from gray to pink, so that

he could see them better. He just looked at me.

"What now?" I asked.

"Um, one, your spines just changed color."

"And…?"

"And that's… normal… for you?"

"Yes."

"Alright." He said. "Two, what in the name of King

Arrik the First is a jeed? Or an aught?" I sighed.

"These are my jeeds," I said, flapping them. "And

these," I sent a pulse of orange shooting down my aughts, "are

my aughts."

"Oh," he said, sounding more like a meatball than a

human being. "See, normally we call that—" he pointed at my

jeed— "a wing, and those things you call autters—"

"Aughts."

"—aughts, we call spines."

I looked at him with derision.

"Why should I care what people call dragon body parts?"

Dibbins didn't seem to have an answer for that. Well, I *am* intimidating.

"Whatever. Do you know where to sit now?" I huffed.

Without answering, he climbed onto my back again, this time in the proper spot.

"Much better." I told him. "Now we can get out of here!" I started toward the mouth of the cave, preparing to fly out of the top of the crater of Spendidium.

"Where are you going?" Dibbins asked.

"Um, out." I said. "Where did you think I was—"

"Wait. I didn't realize we wouldn't be using my tunnel. I need to get my digging machine first; we'll need it to break into the dwarves' tunnels." He slid off my back and dashed down the hole he had made busting into my cave. A moment later I heard

him grunting, and more of the clanking noises I'd heard earlier,

and then a machine started appearing through the hole.

I say it started appearing because this thing was *big*. And

complicated. I could see a large curved piece of metal at the

front that I assumed did the digging, but after that I was lost.

There were strings and gears and what appeared to be a fan

(There was one in my cousin Stegrallian's hoard. He's very

fond of human technology) and a myriad of other things, all on

a rolling platform. Finally, Dibbins' head emerged from the

tunnel, and he crawled out.

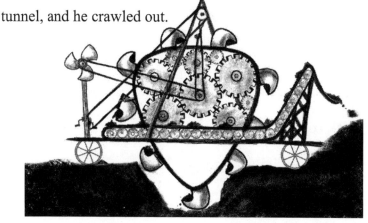

[Fig. 3, Dibbins' Digging Machine]

"So, do you think we can take this with us?" He asked. I eyed it uncertainly.

"It's certainly complex, isn't it?" I managed.

"Well, of course!" he said. "It's top-of-the-line! The best there is. Naturally it's complex. This little baby," he patted the heap of metal and other stuff fondly, "Has over a hundred and twenty moving parts. The old model only had ninety-three."

"And that's... good?" I asked.

"Of course it's good!" He exclaimed. I looked over the machine again rather dubiously.

"It seems like it would break pretty easily." I said. He looked at me like I was missing something obvious.

"Of course it does, that's why it's so expensive!" I didn't understand, and he could tell. "Look, the more complex technology is, the better it is, right?" He didn't give me a chance to answer, which annoyed me. No one rhetorical-questions *me…* but I was sort of interested in his warped sense of logic, so I let it go.

"Now, if the technology is better it will naturally cost more. Then, because it is so complicated, it will break more often, and you pay lots of money to have it fixed. That's how you know the machine you've got is a good one, if it costs you a lot. The more you pay, the better the machine."

I blinked a few times, but that was all I could think of in terms of a response. Humans are all plagued with a terrible case of the dumb about some things; apparently technology is one of them.

"Can you make it any more compact?" I asked. "It'll be awfully hard to fly with that… thing… strung out across my back."

"Sure," Dibbins said, and set about folding the thing up. It didn't actually take too long, and by the time he finished the whole machine fit into a bag I hadn't noticed him carrying before. He slung the bag over his shoulders, groaning about the weight, and climbed onto my back one more time.

"Alright," I said, "are we off?"

"Yes!" Dibbins practically shouted. I launched us out of the cave and let myself fall until we were almost above the lava.

"*Iz!*" Dibbins shouted. Laughing at the terror I'd inspired (I was not about to dump him to his doom, let's be real, I'm not completely awful) I spread my jeeds and flew up into the evening sky.

CHAPTER THREE

"I thought adventures were supposed to be perilous and slow, and you were only supposed to get there—wherever 'there' may be—after some arduous journey that tests your strength and resolve." I complained. "So how come we're already here?" Dibbins slid off my back as I looked around. When he'd told me the dwarves' mountain was near the volcano, I hadn't realized just how near. The moon had only risen a few hours earlier, and we had arrived. I was appalled. I was also tired to the bones, but I wasn't about to tell Dibbins that.

"Well, not all adventures are the same. And it's not over yet." A strangely dark look crossed his face.

"Eh?"

"Well, we still have to break in, get the treasure, and break out." His expression was clear again, and I wondered if I had misread it at first. Human faces are tricky, being so unbelievably tiny.

"That's true," I said, "but not until morning." I yawned. Dibbins looked around.

"Shouldn't we find a safer place to sleep?" He asked.

"Why?"

"There are wild animals in the mountains, and—" he stopped. With the look I was giving him I couldn't have gotten my thoughts across more clearly than if I had been holding a sign reading, "I'M A DRAGON, YOU IDIOT."

"Right." Dibbins said. "Dragon. Well, let's find somewhere to rest then."

So Dibbins and I found a stand of trees that I would fit under. He pulled bread and cheese and meat out of his bag, and I gathered all the rocks within reach.

"Iz?" Dibbins asked. "It's kind of cold. Do you think you could…" I nabbed the nearest branch and laid it on the ground between us. Then I breathed some flame onto it. It lit immediately.

"That will burn until morning." I told Dibbins.

"Thanks."

We finished eating. I curled my krane around one tree and the rest of me around another. Dibbins stretched out by the fire with his head on his arm.

"Good night, Iz." He said.

"Night, Dibbins." I settled down onto the ground and stared at the dragon fire as it sizzled, burning hot and slow. I wondered if Mother had found my note, and if she was worried about me. I thought about how angry Mooninga would be that I'd gone adventuring without her. Eventually, though, my eyelids got heavy, and bit by bit, I fell asleep.

The next morning was overcast and rabbitty. Yes, I said rabbity. I woke blearily, opening one eye at a time. That is to say, when I opened the first eye and registered what I was seeing, I jumped into a sort of sitting position as I opened the other eye.

It was so *cute*. The fuzzball with eyes that I'd seen in that first sleepy glance turned out to be a little gray rabbit. It sniffed at me so fearlessly that I was taken aback; first Dibbins, then this fluffy creature? Was I not as scary as I thought?

Nah, that wasn't it.

Dibbins stirred when I sat up. He muttered something like, "This doesn't make sense, Haze..." before he woke up fully and remembered where he was. He sat up too, and rubbed his eyes.

"Iz?" He asked, "is something wrong?"

"Rabbit," I crooned. It was so cute, inching toward me with curiosity. It chattered at me, and somewhere in the heart of my magic (are we being serious right now? Of course I have magic. All dragons do. Honestly…) I heard an echo of words.

"Excellent," Dibbins was saying behind me. Then I stopped paying attention to him and focused on the rabbit and the magic, so all I caught after that was "mumble, something, yadda, stew."

You ask the silliest questions. Of course that's not what he *actually* said.

Anyway, listening to my magic, I addressed the rabbit.

"Pardon me, could you say that again?" It looked at me, its large, reflective eyes wide.

"Momma," it moaned. I understood now. "Where's Momma?" I didn't know the answer to that, and sighed. As I did, a smidgeon of fire shot out of my nostrils—just a tiny bit, and it was nowhere near the rabbit, but he looked terrified. "Momma!" The little rabbit squealed and hopped with a thump up into the air, then landed, staring at the place where my fire had been. "Momma, fire eats," he said mournfully. I looked at him for a moment, confused—the way kids (and other species' young ones) talk has always confused me—then realized in a heartrending moment that this little rabbit's mother must have been cooked in front of him. As I looked at the fuzzbutt, I saw Dibbins come around behind the rabbit with a net.

"Good, Iz," he said, "keep him mesmerized and I'll catch him for breakfast." It took me a moment to process what Dibbins had said, as I had to switch languages to do it. When I did, my head snapped up.

"No." I said. I extended a fiing to the little rabbit, who had twisted around, seen Dibbins, and was shaking with fear. "I'm keeping him." Dibbins looked at me in disbelief.

"I didn't think dragons kept pets," he said derisively.

"Well, I'm keeping this one," I said flatly. Then I made the leap in my mind to rabbit language and addressed the trembling furball who was, for the first time, looking at me with terror. "What's your name, little one?" I asked him. He stared at me for a moment.

"Zeeim." He said finally. I felt like he would have been crying from stress and fear and sorrow, but couldn't somehow.

"Well, Zeeim," I said, "I will be your momma now." Zeeim blinked once, twice, then shuffled to rest against my forearm.

"Momma." He said in what I felt sure was a rabbit's version of a sob. Gently I stroked his head with a fiing—his head was so small! Then, remembering Dibbins, I looked up. He was staring.

"What?" I said.

"That seemed very… tender. What did you say to it?"

"You hush, meatball." I said. It suddenly occurred to me how Dibbins probably saw me: a treasure-obsessed rogue without a lot of feelings but with plenty of sass. Which, to be fair, was kind of how I saw him. I wondered momentarily if he was not quite that way either. My thoughts were interrupted by Zeeim knocking his head against me. I glanced down and saw that he was staring in fear at Dibbins. Carefully I lifted Zeeim, then pointed at his fuzzy chest. Realizing that, if I was to be his momma, he should learn to speak Dracogin (dragon language, if you didn't catch that) rather than Rabbit, I spoke in my native tongue.

"Zeeim." I said clearly. He nodded. Then I pointed at Dibbins. "Dibbins." After a moment Zeeim nodded again. Then he looked at me ponderously and pointed with a paw. I thought for a moment. "Iz." I said. "Momma." Then I explained the difference, first in Dracogin, then in Rabbit.

All this made me realize something. I looked at Dibbins.

"Dibbins? I'm speaking Dracogin. How are we communicating?" Dibbins looked uncomfortable.

"One of my ancestors did a favor for a dragon who lived near his, um, house. In gratitude, the dragon blessed him and all of his family forever with the ability to speak Dracogin as well as our ancestral language," he said. I nodded at this. The ancestor must have lived long ago if the dragon had willingly associated with humans—the last tale like that that I knew of was the skirmish where the great king Roppax defended his human friend, King something-or-other, against some other unimportant human king. That had led to one of the wars between the humans, and dragons in general had decided that the wisest course of action was to keep their distance from the two-legs. But the story was plausible; dragon magic lasts a long time.

Are you surprised by that story? Hey! Just because we look like killing machines doesn't mean we're out to destroy every other living creature. Get over your biases!

Zeeim nudged me again. I looked at him, and he spoke—in Dracogin, to my pleased surprise.

"We go home?" He asked. "Momma go home? Zeeim go home?" I shook my head at him.

"Not yet, Zeeim. First we have to finish some… errands." Zeeim nodded glumly. "Then we will go home. To a new home, Zeeim. You will like it." It occurred to me that Zeeim would have trouble finding rabbit friends in Spendidium, but that was a concern for a different occasion.

"Dibbins," I said, "will you help me make a sling for Zeeim to ride in? Then we can go see about the dwarves."

"A carrying sling?" He said, sounding horrified. "But Iz, we haven't studied nearly enough to build a high-class one. I know almost nothing about modern safety standards."

"Is this more of that technology bilge you were spewing earlier?"

"No, this is about safety. If something is going to be safe it has to be scrutinized inch by inch by scientists who understand these things. And it should expire quickly." I rolled my eyes.

"Dibbins, just help me build a bag with a wide, flat bottom and a hole to see out of that can be strapped around my body." Grumbling, he complied, using a large blanket that appeared out of his bag—which I was beginning to suspect was magical, to hold so much. Putting off that suspicion, I helped Dibbins attach the sack. Then I scooped Zeeim into it.

"Is that alright, Zeeim?" I asked.

"Uh-huh."

[Fig. 4, Zeeim]

"Do you need anything before we go? To relieve yourself? Some food?" Dibbins stared at me, amazed (I supposed) by the way I looked after Zeeim. Since I'd have preferred him to think of me as terrifying and awesome, this was a bit annoying. Eventually I told him to stop staring and gather some clover for Zeeim, which he did with a smirk.

Finally we were all prepared—Dibbins' sack packed, plan worked out, digging machine in place. Zeeim was happily nibbling clover in the bag beneath me. Dibbins was cheerfully cranking up the machine, and I was watching him do it in fascination. I was struck again by how ridiculous the contraption was, with its many moving pieces. Most of them looked unnecessary as well. At last, Dibbins turned around.

"I think that should be enough cranking for it to dig all the way in; the tunnel behind this part of the mountain is very close."

"How do you know that?" I asked.

"Old maps." He said vaguely.

"How did you get those?" I asked, curious. Dibbins shifted, looking uncomfortable.

"The library." He said.

"Must be some library," I replied. Dibbins seemed very strange to me. I wondered if he wasn't some ordinary thief, as I had thought, but rather some master thief over a clan of them or something.

"Tell me about yourself, Dibbins," I said as the human bent over his machine. He stood back up and looked at me in surprise.

"Well, I'm a robber of evil dwarves. Clearly."

"Come on, there aren't enough dwarves in the area to make that a full-time job. I doubt there are enough dwarves in all of Daiines to make that a full-time job, let alone *evil* dwarves. I'm not stupid. Spill." I said.

Dibbins sighed. "Does it matter?" He asked.

"I suppose not," I said, "I'm just curious. How did you come by top-of-the-line—" (that last was said soaking in sarcasm)—"machinery, and old maps of secret dwarven halls?" Dibbins moved uncomfortably again.

"I stole those too, okay?" He demanded. I might have questioned further, but right then the digging machine started emitting a pink smoke.

"Oh, no," Dibbins said, catching sight of it. "A break in the alignment coordinating processor." He indicated something that looked like a rubber-band ball (no, I didn't know what a rubber-band ball was then, but I've since learned.) "This will take hours to fix properly." He groaned loudly, making Zeeim jump in his pouch.

"Nonsense," I said, inspecting the soft dirt of the mountain wall. "Clean up that…creation. I'll take care of this." I extended the fiings on my front snop fully, then started clawing at the dirt. I felt Dibbins' shocked eyes on me as he banged the machine together. I guess he hadn't realized that I could do this.

Dumb, Dibbins. Dumb.

And you, you reading this, did you think I could? Huh?

Oh.

Well okay, you're smarter than Dibbins was being that day.

Anyway, it took me about five minutes to blast through to the interior tunnel. I cleared a hole big enough for me to pass through, then whispered to Dibbins.

"Don't you think they'll notice this?" I asked. It was, of course, a pretty big hole.

"Yeah, eventually," Dibbins said with a grin. I shrugged in confusion, then followed him into the tunnels of the evil dwarves.

CHAPTER FOUR

Imagine you're in a tunnel underground without any torches or enchanted stones to light your way. Put your hand up right in front of your face; you can't see it in the darkness. Now, if you were enough of a dork to actually put your hand in front of your face, go ahead and bop yourself on the nose with it. The point is, the tunnels were dark. Really, really dark. Even growing up in and out of caves, my sense of direction was useless without anything to see by at all (dragons usually have fires burning around their caves.) I even walked into a wall— you can consider your nose-bopping a parallel to that if you're still trying to share in my experience. Finally, Dibbins and I stopped. Actually, I stopped, and he stepped on my krane (ask your friend to kick you in the behind if you want to know what *that* felt like.) *Then* he stopped.

"Iz," he whispered, "can you use some fire to help us see? Or some magic?" I sighed. Breathing fire continuously is exhausting and not especially healthy. And I didn't know the magic to make light. I debated internally, and had nearly reached the conclusion that fire was the only answer when I heard Zeeim's little voice from below me, speaking in Rabbit.

"Mamma! Big fall! Ouch! Don't step!"

"What?" I asked.

"See big fall? Don't step!" Cautiously I breathed out a bit of flame and started in surprise. To my left was a chasm deeper than even I wanted to contemplate. Somehow Zeeim had seen it. Quickly I translated for Dibbins, who looked thoughtful.

"Rabbits spend most of their time underground, especially when they're young. Very likely Zeeim can see in the dark far better than either of us," he said. I smiled.

"I told you he shouldn't be breakfast," I gloated.

"Yeah, yeah. Can he help us?"

"Zeeim?" I asked, careful to use Dracogin, "can you help Momma? I can't see in the dark as well as you can." There was a scrambling and I heard his voice, now unmuffled, his head outside the sling.

"Yup!" I reached under myself and scooped up the little rabbit—he really was very small, and had to be very young—and plopped him onto my head. His weight barely made a difference. He clung to me and shivered from fear.

"Zeeim, can you hold on?"

"Yup," he said through chattering teeth.

"Good," I told him. "Now can you help Momma and Dibbins find our way to light?"

Our journey became a good deal safer after that. Zeeim would pat my head on the side he wanted me to turn to, and I would relay the directions in a whisper. We continued for an hour before Zeeim decided that he needed food and a nap. As he had helped us a great deal, and really was quite young, we stopped. Zeeim climbed back into his pouch and munched on clover while I tore a rock out of the wall to snack on (a much lighter flavor than I was used to,) and Dibbins pulled some kind of fruit out of his sack.

Zeeim napped, but Dibbins and I couldn't sleep. I think the darkness made us both uncomfortable; it felt so eternal that we had already lost track of time, and if my feet hadn't been on the floor I would hardly have known which way was up. So it was with relief that we heard Zeeim's soft voice when he woke.

We continued on like that for two more meals before I started to wonder if we were even under the right mountain.

"Dibbins," I said, restraining the frustration in my voice—well, mostly, anyway, "why have we not come to any lighted areas yet? This is ridiculous. Even dwarves use some light." Dibbins sighed.

"I don't know, Iz. I knew this part of the tunnels was abandoned, but I didn't think it was so large. My maps were very old…" I would have stared at him in astonishment—you know, if I could see him at all.

"So this all might just be a wild goat chase?" I barely kept my voice from breaking. Even dragons have fears. I was beginning to realize that I had a keen dislike for absolute dark. I felt like it was pressing in on me from all sides. If I had been alone, I would have lost my mind. I ached for the dragon-fire-lit walls of my home cave. The only real comfort to me came from the furry warmth sitting on top of my head, gently tapping one side or the other to give me direction. Even with Zeeim, I was starting to feel the strain of a darkness that crouched in every corner and assaulted me at every turn.

"No," Dibbins answered, "I know the dwarves are under this mountain."

"How?"

"I know, and that's enough." Dibbins snapped.

"Don't you dare talk to me like that," I snarled. My nerves had been pushed way past fraying, and I was not willing to let this little brunch on sticks push me around for a second longer. Flame spewed out of my mouth in raw frustration.

Several things happened then.

First, light filled the tunnel we were treading. As it did, I felt myself relax just a bit—there was still light in the world.

Second, Dibbins shouted and dodged the fire, for which I was eventually grateful—just then I still wanted to roast him.

Third, the combined noise of my roar and his shout knocked some rocks loose. Pebbles and slightly larger appetizers rolled down toward us, bouncing off my scales with a musical sound. It wasn't anything to worry about; not a full-scale rockslide or anything.

You know, at first.

We ran for it. Dibbins actually passed me up because he could run more freely in the confined space. Eventually the sound of falling rock faded behind us, but as Dibbins stopped to gasp for air (dragons never gasp for air) a new sound filled the tunnel.

Drums.

Now, I've read a fair number of adventure stories. I studied the old legends and myths in school and I enjoyed them enough to pay attention. I particularly liked stories about dwarves, because they were so dragon-like in their love of treasures. But I'd learned that if you are underground in a dwarven city and you hear drums, it will probably not go well. To say the least. The exit behind us was blocked by the results of the rockslide. Zeeim was shaking so badly that I thought his fur might start flying off.

"Dibbins?" I said tentatively, lifting Zeeim back into his safe sling. "This does not look good for us."

"No." Dibbins agreed.

There was one bright spot in the situation—and I mean that literally: moments later lights appeared at the end of the tunnel. Even in my stress about the drumming of doom I couldn't help feeling relief at seeing those lights. They came nearer and nearer to us until we could see that the light came from torches. The firelight, so bright compared to the black night we had been experiencing, fell onto the faces of its bearers. Dwarves. And they didn't look too happy to see us.

[Fig. 5, Dwarf]

They smelled like dirt. I don't mean that in an insulting and figurative way. They smelled, quite literally, like soil. I thought this might be because they spent so much time digging tunnels in—you guessed it—the dirt. Whatever they smelled like, they were not especially friendly. They sized up Dibbins (taller than them by the length of two adult horns—about two feet in human measurements,) then they sized up *me*. One of them, a fellow with a massive beard spread all around his face, grunted to the others. From my practice with Zeeim it wasn't difficult to switch my mind over to Dwarf speech.

"Get the magic," Bigbeard said. Another dwarf to Bigbeard's left pulled out a bottle of something powdered and sparkly. I focused in on it, mesmerized by the shininess. The dwarf took out the cork in the neck of the bottle, and the powder rose into the air. It formed a ring around my head. That didn't strike me as good. My vision started to go dark in spots, and finally all I could see was blackness again.

***

When I came to, I heard a muffled grunting noise. I blinked excessively and my vision started to clear—the blackness faded in spots just like it had come. When I could finally see again I completely forgot about the grunting noise.

Shiny. So shiny.

The room was packed with treasure. Shelves and trunks stuffed full, goblets and rings strung from strands of pearls and gems. I wondered at first if it was magicked to disappear when someone unauthorized touched it, but I was lying across a heap of gold coins and nothing had happened yet—to me or the loot. I sighed, content, and stretched out on my back.

"Momma? Momma, you up?" Came a soft voice. I turned my head. Zeeim was bouncing on his hind feet next to me. I sat up.

"Yes, I'm up," I said to him.

"Good. Dibby all stuck," he said. I snorted, then decided to keep to myself that Zeeim referred to Dibbins as "Dibby." I looked around. The muffled noise that had woken me had come from Dibbins as he struggled with his gag. He was bound with what I thought was a superfluous amount of rope to a throne that was made of precious metals and decorated with emeralds and sapphires. I was sort of jealous. Dragons don't get thrones.

"Zeeim," I said, "will you help Dibbins out of his ropes? I bet you can bite through them. My teeth are too big," I said, showing them. Zeeim automatically flinched a little at the sight of my massive knoppers, but he hopped over to Dibbins with a good will.

"I bite," he said in Dracogin. Then he started gnawing on the rope binding Dibbins' hands. He chewed for a few moments and the whole bunch of rope came apart.

"Thank you," Dibbins said to me after he'd removed his gag.

"Don't thank me," I said, "I would have chopped you in half. Thank Zeeim." Dibbins eyed the rabbit for a moment, looking doubtful. Then he plunked down into a squat, looked Zeeim in the eye, and said,

"Thank you, Zeeim. I couldn't have gotten free without you." Zeeim twisted around shyly, washed a whisker with a paw, and bounded back over to me.

Fig. 6, Treasure Cave]

"Not that it would have made much difference," Dibbins said.

"What?" I asked.

"If you had chopped me in half, Iz. You've already as good as killed me, getting us stuck here." I couldn't believe my ears (actually, as reptiles, dragons don't have ears in the mammalian sense. Rather we have ear*holes*. So I couldn't believe my earholes.) Dibbins was accusing *me* of getting us trapped?

"It was your idea to go on this stupid expedition anyway, you know!" I growled. Dibbins glared.

"Well if you hadn't roared and brought all the dwarves running, my plan would have been fine!"

"They used magic against us! You didn't plan for *that*, did you? And you should have!" Bits of flame were dripping out of my mouth in an unsteady stream, I was so livid. I had just enough presence of mind to turn my head away from Zeeim, so he wouldn't catch fire.

"They wouldn't have had time to use magic if you had just attacked like you were supposed to! What's the good of having a dragon if they won't even fight off the enemy?" Dibbins was shouting. I was shouting, too. Zeeim was cowering.

"HAVE a dragon? You don't HAVE a dragon! A dragon came along with you, but I don't belong to you! Humans have never been able to enslave dragons, and they never will! Of all the arrogant, pretentious, rude species, yours is the worst!" I turned and moved to the back wall, facing away from stupid Dibbins and his stupid arguing. He had started this whole troublesome shenanigan. It was his fault, not mine. So there.

So there we were, each trying hard to pretend the other didn't exist. If I could've left the cave right then and there, I would have. I know Dibbins felt the same way. But it was just too *shiny*, and besides, going outside would mean our deaths—

the dwarves were right outside the door, keeping watch. But mostly it was the shine, the luster of the treasure, that kept me from trying to escape.

(Yeah, you've read that paragraph before, it's the part from the beginning. I told you this part of the story was more exciting than the first bit.)

Zeeim bounced along after me once the shouting match—which I had totally won—had ended.

"Momma?" He said in his soft way.

"Yes, Zeeim?" I sighed.

"Hungry."

"Eat some clover, then." I told him.

"All gone." I looked at him. He was serious; he'd eaten all of the clover Dibbins had gathered for him. How do you explain to a baby rabbit that he needs to conserve his food? Unwillingly, I called out to Dibbins.

"Do you have anything that can pass as rabbit food? Zeeim is hungry."

"Tell him to eat the clover, then!"

"He finished it."

"Oh." I heard Dibbins reach around in his sack. "Here, Zeeim." He said. I turned my head just enough to see Dibbins offering a carrot to Zeeim. The little rabbit bounced over to Dibbins and grabbed the carrot in his teeth, then settled down to munch on it.

"So ends the kingdom of Lethina," Dibbins muttered bitterly.

"What?" I asked.

"This treasure, it was going to save my kingdom," he sighed. "No treasure, no chance."

"Explain." I said briskly. "Now." I turned around to face him as he started talking.

"I'm Prince Arrik the eighteenth of the kingdom of Lethina," he said, jerking his thumb behind him to indicate that it was nearby. "I'm my parents' second son. My brother, the heir, is visiting an ally two months away by horse, leaving me to worry about the kingdom's future." He laughed bitterly. "Our neighbors, the kingdom of Carobinn, declared war on us six months ago. We thought we could handle it; they have more soldiers, but we had much better finances and planned to hire mercenaries. But the Carobinns were smart. They hired these dwarves—" he gestured around the cave— "to rob us of our wealth. All of it. Our treasuries, our banks—everything is empty. The mercenaries wouldn't stay for free, so our tiny army is standing against their huge one. My father has all but resigned himself to being conquered, but I *refuse* to accept the end of Lethina. I decided to steal the treasure back. That's when I started collecting old maps of these tunnels, bought the digging machine, and sneaked away. I thought I could break into this chamber by myself—it is pretty close to the edge of the mountain—and steal it all back. I was nearly caught trying. So I went back to the maps and found the route the two—the *three* of us took. Then I went searching for someone strong enough to get me in and out.

"I had heard rumors about a treasure-obsessed young dragon living by the volcano Ithnitt—the one you call Spendidium. So I drilled in to what I thought was an empty cave. I got lucky, I found you on my second try."

"What was your first try?" I asked, interrupting.

"I attempted to climb to the top of the mountain. I thought I'd come in from above. I came up the wrong place, though, there was lava everywhere, I couldn't go past it."

"It's pretty much like that everywhere," I commented.

"Well, then I realized that I had my digging machine with me. I checked my maps of the dragon caves of Ithnitt— they're old maps, but your cave seemed too small to live in—"

"It is."

"—so I drilled in. And there you were." He broke off from his story and bent to pet Zeeim's soft head as he slept off his meal.

"Wait, Dibbins, how did you know who the thieves were in the first place?"

"A spy. A runaway dwarf, actually, from Coortain."

"Ah." I couldn't think of what to say.

"We'll have to find a way out of here soon," Dibbins—Prince Arrik, although I stuck with "Dibbins"—said. "It's all well and good for you, Iz, eating rocks, but Zeeim and I… Iz? I have an idea." He sounded as though he were trying to keep too much excitement from leaking out of his voice.

"What is it?

"Are you hungry?" He asked.

"I guess," I answered. I hadn't thought about it, but there was space in my stomach for something crunchy. "I've never eaten this kind of rock, though." I looked around. The whole back wall appeared to be stones with bits of soil packed between them.

"Do you think you can?"

"I don't see why not."

"Good. Let's load you up with treasure. You've got a big meal ahead of you, and I want to bring along as much stuff on the way out as I can."

It took me a minute to catch on to Dibbins' plan. It was solid lunacy. But if we pulled it off right, we would have so much treasure that we could stop his war and start my hoard and be remembered for it for many, many years.

Dibbins, as it turns out, had stuffed his magically weightless bag with more magically weightless bags. The charm would make the contents of the pack seem almost nonexistent for a while, and we could pack in a good load after that. I knew I could carry it all.

Dragon. Just a reminder.

The difficulty came in strapping the bags to my back. Finally in desperation we cut apart Zeeim's sling and used the straps to secure the bags. Zeeim looked very upset until I assured him that he could sit up on my back with Dibbins to hold onto him.

"Just a few more," Dibbins said, "and we'll have enough for both of us." I nodded. I was excited. My own hoard, my own treasures! Plus Dibbins' kingdom would be saved. He seemed to think that was the most important thing, bless his little heart.

There came, suddenly, the sound of footsteps approaching the door, then of keys singing as they smacked into each other while the door unlocked. Dibbins and I looked at each other in fear.

"Run!" Dibbins said. "Eat! I'll grab Zeeim and catch up." He picked up a sword that had been, until that moment, waiting to be bagged. I didn't feel especially comfortable about the idea of abandoning the other two, especially Zeeim, but I was our best way out. I turned my back to Dibbins and my attention to the wall of stones. Using my snopps, I pried out a large stone from the middle of the wall and ate it. Then I did it again. And again. And again.

The rocks had a very different taste than the ones at home. Less spicy, more meaty. I wondered if that was good or bad, and the effect it would have on my flame—dragon fire comes from the kinds of rock they eat. Volcano dwellers are good flamers because they eat volcanic rocks all the time.

I thought about all of this as I chomped into the wall. Suddenly I realized the obvious solution to the predicament we were in, and I turned around to face the fray. Dibbins was doing well, although I supposed that came from training as a prince. He was fighting three dwarves and all three were bleeding, although so was Dibbins. Zeeim was in a corner, his eyes shut, and he was jumping at every metal-on-metal sound.

"Duck, Dibbins!" I roared. He dropped to the floor, hands over his head. The dwarves looked around in surprise (dwarves are not awesome enough to speak Dracogin) as I opened my mouth wide to roast them. I caught sight of Zeeim shuddering in the corner and changed my mind.

"Dibbins, grab Zeeim!" Dibbins looked around, scooped up my rabbit baby, and scuttled around to stand behind me. He was smart enough to cover Zeeim's face, too—I didn't want him to see Mamma hurting anyone, even if they were evil. I turned back to the confused dwarves, who were edging toward me. As I opened my mouth again, I saw the one in the back grab another bottle full of a sparkly liquid from inside his hood. *Not this time,* I thought. Using the intense firepower I had been born with, I rained down flame on them.

Dwarves have a natural resistance to heat. They have to, working near the world's heart like they do. Even so, a good spray of dragonfire will eventually take them out. The two in front were unconscious when the third dwarf got the stopper out of his magic bottle. He splashed me with the contents. A smell of dirty socks and bananas filled the room.

I coughed.

No fire came out of my mouth.

The dwarf (the one that was still awake) looked very satisfied with himself. So naturally I grabbed him in my front snop and dangled him by his robes in front of me.

"What have you done to me?" I roared. I paused briefly to appreciate the way the cave amplified my voice, which was already super intimidating, if I may say so. (What a silly expression for a dragon to use; who's going to stop me from saying so if I want to?) Then I focused back on the dwarf. "Speak up," I continued, "you really want to tell me." I smiled my deadliest smile at him, showing all my shiny knoppers. He shivered in fear. Ha, ha.

"Just a bit of magic," the dwarf muttered. "It will wear off by sunset, I promise!" He squealed on the last few words.

"Alright. I'll let you live." I said. Then I dropped him. (He was going to be fine after a brutal headache. I thought you might care.) One of the other dwarves stirred slightly. I growled at him, and he froze.

"Now, Dibbins, let's get out of here," I said. Zeeim was trembling again, so I took him from Dibbins and cradled him, stroking his soft fur. "It's alright, Zeeim," I said quietly. "Momma didn't hurt the evil dwarves. Not much, anyway." Zeeim snuggled against me, which I took as a sign of his forgiveness.

Bruueee!! I heard a squeal from behind me. Whipping around, I saw that the dwarf who had come to was blowing some kind of safety whistle, signaling the other dwarves to come take us down.

Dibbins darted forward and smacked him in the head so hard that he was knocked out. Again.

"We've really got to hurry now, Iz," Dibbins said frantically.

"Right." I turned back to the wall I had been devouring. I'd made a fair-sized dent in it before I turned the dwarves into roasted marshmallows. "Help me dig out rocks, Dibbins." I said.

"Me too?" Zeeim asked, squirming to get out of my clutch and onto the ground.

"Sure, Zeeim, you too. Dig the big rocks out for Momma." I didn't expect him to be good at it, which was silly of me. Rabbits spend their lives digging, so he went at the lower rocks and freed them faster than even I did. Dibbins pulled them out for him (they were often bigger than Zeeim's whole body) and I ate them. All three of us were pulling rocks out as fast as we could, and I ate them as fast as possible.

"We could just toss the rocks," I said, feeling full.

"Sorry, Iz," Dibbins said. "I'm afraid if we do that something in here will break."

"So?"

"So there's a protection charm on the treasure in here," he said. "The dwarves didn't think anybody could get in *and* get out, so they didn't bother cursing it against theft. Which just shows you the brilliance of dwarf logic. But they use this room to keep prisoners in, as it's guarded better than any other rooms anyway. They were afraid an angry captive might destroy their valuables out of spite."

"So what happens if something breaks?" I asked, curious in spite of myself and the rush we were in.

"The treasure vanishes and the cave collapses."

"It just vanishes?"

"Well, technically, any treasure under this roof transports to a different cave."

"And what about this one? It's their best-protected room and they'd just destroy it? That seems a bit wasteful." I said between mouthfuls of stone.

"Iz, they're dwarves. They could just re-dig this room in a day or two."

"Right."

Two things happened in the same moment. Zeeim started squealing and Dibbins started shouting. Zeeim was squealing because he'd just broken through to the other side (that's my boy!) Dibbins shouted because a back-up guard of dwarves had just appeared in the doorway.

I growled. Adventurers apparently don't get a lot of time to rest. There was still too much stone between us and the open air to safely break through; we needed a plan. Immediately.

"Dibbins!" I yelled over his own noise. "The treasure in the bags, how does it weigh nothing?"

"Trans-dimensional shifting!" he shouted back. Trans-what now?

"Does that mean it's not technically under the roof of this cavern?"

"I—*guess!*" he shouted, hurling a rock at the dwarves, who seemed to be planning how best to deal with us.

"Grab the throne out of the bag nearest you. Smash it!" I shouted. He looked at me curiously for an instant, then I saw understanding dawn on his face. As the dwarves charged into the treasure room, their treasure all vanished and the roof of the cave began immediately to collapse over their heads. Zeeim, Dibbins, and I had formed a sort of smaller cave out of the way of the cave-in that protected us. A mountain of stone collected in the middle of what had been the treasure room a moment earlier. There were screams from the dwarves, but they could barely be heard over the sound of the falling rocks. I hoped little Zeeim couldn't hear them (probably a vain hope, with his ears.)

As the pile grew on the floor of the cavern, it started to spread out in all directions, including toward us. Like a wave of lava, it was rushing toward us to bring death.

"Dig!" Dibbins and I shouted at the same time. We tore small boulders out of the wall, and I swallowed them—there was no other place for us to put them. Finally we made a hole big enough for both of us (Zeeim having sensibly leaped out his small hole and away from danger) to go through. Then we both climbed out into the sunlight, fleeing the steady onslaught of stone. Gathering up Zeeim as I sprinted by, Dibbins and I fled up the hill next to us into a copse of trees.

"Dibbins," I said, "thanks."

"For what?"

"You could've left me on my own in there. You didn't. So thanks." Dibbins nodded.

"You're welcome. And, you know, thanks for getting us out."

I nodded, then collapsed on the ground, feeling very,

very full.

CHAPTER FIVE

It was afternoon when we charged out of the mountain, but we fell asleep, exhausted. I didn't get a lot of rest though; I had nightmares filled with the screams of dwarves. When I woke up, just as the sun was starting to set, I shook Dibbins.

"Dibbins!" I said. "Do you know that those dwarves were really evil? I mean, were they worse than just being thieves? Did they… did we do a good thing for the world, letting them get hurt or die?" Dibbins opened his mouth to answer, then glanced up.

"I'll tell you all about them, Iz, but we have to get out of here."

"Why?"

"Because the rest of the dwarves will want revenge. They're going to come chasing after us." I realized why he was so suddenly worried: the dwarves, unaccustomed to almost any light, would never choose to come out into the sun. It not only burned their skin—sometimes so much that the skin became hard and flaky—but usually made them blind, and sometimes melted their soft ears so that they collapsed and made the dwarf deaf. After nightfall, though, they often came out—to gather food and metal that was not found in their own halls (and in the case of this clan, to rob neighboring kingdoms.) If we stayed this close to the dwarves' mountain after the sunset, we would be in for a serious battle.

Sunset... I tentatively breathed a bit of fire. It shot out of my mouth almost as well as normal, and I suspected the reason it didn't work like it usually would was all the strange rocks I'd been eating. It was, if not *exceptional* fire-breathing, at least good fire-breathing.

"Well, that's back to normal at least," I muttered to myself. Then I addressed Dibbins: "Get on my back. Do you still have your bag?"

"Yes."

"And the treasure is in place?"

"Of course."

"Good." I turned to my downy charge. "Zeeim, you ride with Dibbins, okay? He will hold onto you so you don't fall off Mamma's back?"

"Okay." Zeeim sounded much cheerier than I had expected; I guess he'd forgiven Dibbins for wanting to make him into stew when they first met.

"Good. Thank you, Zeeim. Dibbins—"

"We go home now?" Zeeim asked. I sighed.

"Not yet Zeeim, I'm sorry." He hung his head. "We're going to go visit some friends, okay?"

"Friends?" His tone lightened.

"Yes, we will go make some new friends, okay?"

"Okay. I ride with Dibby."

"Good job, sweetheart." I reflected for a moment that Zeeim was doing a very good job understanding a lot of Dracogin; I barely had to translate anything for him, even if he hadn't figured out how to answer everything in the same language. This troubled me a bit; maybe it *was* best if he continued speaking Rabbit, so that one day he could meet other rabbits and communicate with them.

"Iz, we gotta go." Dibbins cut in on my thoughts.

"Right. Mount up." Dibbins picked up Zeeim, then clambered onto my back. I walked out of the trees, then lifted myself into the air. Flying was a little tricky when I was weighed down with so much gold, but I thought it was worth the trouble. I meditated happily on my hoard for a few seconds, then focused on flying. I navigated into a current, where the sound of the wind was less overwhelming and I could glide more easily. Then I called out to Dibbins,

"Alright Dibbins, tell me about the dwarves." He scooted forward on my back a little, but not far enough to get in the way of my jeeds.

"Are you sure you want… little ears to hear this?" I considered. The first thing I considered was that, compared to his body, Zeeim's ears weren't little at all. I pushed that thought away, unwilling to go through the bother of shouting mockery above the sound of the wind—while it had lessened, it still persisted. I thought about what Dibbins meant. Zeeim had apparently seen his mother cooked, so he had some idea of horrors, young as he was. Still, there was no reason to give him more nightmares than he probably already had.

"Tell me in Human," I said.

"Alright." Dibbins paused for a moment, thinking. "The dark dwarves of the mountain Coortain have delved for four centuries into black magic." I shuddered, making Dibbins tip and then yelp. *Nasty* things are done with black magic. Dibbins continued. "It started with a necromancer named In'zdul. Four hundred years ago he took power over the dwarves of Coortain, deposing their king. He's still ruling over them now." I was about to ask why that was suprising. Then I remembered that four hundred years, so brief to a dragon, was generations to dwarves and humans.

"How is he still alive?" I asked instead.

"More black magic," Dibbins said. "He sacrifices a baby dwarf to the dark gods every year under the first full moon that shines over the snow." I almost stopped flying.

"He WHAT?" I didn't care what species, a baby is a baby. I shot such a powerful jet of flame into the air that it actually pushed us backward for a moment.

"IZ!" Dibbins yelled. I flapped some, returning us to the current. Fire was still dripping out between my teeth. I didn't care. I wanted to roast this In'zdul.

Among dragons, life is respected above anything—even treasure. The life of the young, so unused, is considered especially precious. To us, killing a baby would be like... well, actually, humans usually share our views on children. So you should understand my rage.

"I know, Iz," Dibbins said, as if in reaction to my thoughts. He patted me carefully. "He's not going to get away with it for much longer. If we'd known before we would have stopped him then. My father—"

"Arrik the seventeenth?" I guessed. Dibbins laughed.

"No, we're not nearly that well-organized. King Arrik the seventeenth was my great-grandfather. My father is King Roberr the fourteenth. Don't worry about it." He added that last bit after I huffed in annoyance with their stupid system.

"Anyway, my father received intelligence about In'zdul only a few months ago; a dwarf escaped Coortain and reported the whole business to him. We've been trying to decide how to bring In'zdul down since." He broke off suddenly. "Iz, can we fly any lower? I think Zeeim is cold; he won't stop shaking." Then a shocking thing happened.

"Bad dwarf." Zeeim said—in Human. I twisted my head around and saw that Dibbins looked as surprised as I did.

"Dibbins, do all rabbits pick up languages that fast?" I asked, turning my head forward again so that I could dodge the birds flying ahead of me.

"I don't think so," Dibbins said thoughtfully. Then, slowly, he added to Zeeim, "What do you mean, 'bad dwarf?'"

"Bad dwarf," Zeeim said, reverting to Rabbit, which I translated for Dibbins. "Mamma, fire eat." Softly, I responded in the same language.

"Zeeim, do you mean that it was In'zdul who killed your mother?" I had assumed that Zeeim's mother had simply been roasted and eaten by travelers, but now I wasn't sure.

"He's nodding, Iz. And he looks like he wants to cry."

"We're landing." I said. I circled down to a clearing in the woods. Dibbins climbed off of my back and handed Zeeim over to me. The little rabbit curled himself against my bladoon.

"You're safe here," I told Zeeim.

Dibbins didn't continue his story until Zeeim had gone to sleep. Then I asked him,

"So are all of the dwarves evil? Or just—" I glanced at Zeeim—"the one in charge? I mean, if one ran away from him, clearly some of them are alright."

"Not mostly." Dibbins said. "Do you remember I told you we had a spy from Coortain come report to us?" I nodded. "Well, she—the spy—told us that she tried to persuade others to see things as she did. She ran away because they were planning to kill her for heresy."

"Heresy? Isn't that to do with religion?"

"Apparently In'z—apparently the king has led them to believe that his long life is due to his being a god." My jaw dropped. (Literally. That expression originally came from dragons, whose jaws actually drop when they are surprised; it's an inherited trait. The part of our brain that processes surprise is next to the part that takes care of jaw motor control, and when the surprised part expands it nudges the jaw part. There's your draconian neural anatomy lesson for the day.) Nobody got away with claiming godhood for long; the true gods always strike them down.

"How is he still alive?" I asked.

"Further magic." Dibbins said. "He sacrifices animals to the Gods. I'm guessing that that's how Zeeim's mother died."

"To keep a murderer safe from the wrath of the gods?" I kept my fire in check so as not to set Zeeim aflame. I was amazed that even the dark gods accepted his sacrifices. That was some horrible magic.

I beg your pardon? You were doing so *well* at not interrupting, I was—okay, fine. I'll explain.

Our world was originally run by a Council on High, who lived in a palace on clouds that floated above the world. It's far, but it's been visited by dragons a few times. The Council is comprised of the first male and female of every intelligent species—all the ones that have a language of their own—that have been blessed with immortality. In exchange, these gods were charged with the duty of watching over the world and keeping peace and goodness prevalent. No one knows exactly who gave the gods their task, but he lived before the gods of our world, and according to legend, created this world.

A few hundred years later, a revolution separated the gods. Some of them wanted to tighten their authority over the peoples of the world, to gain power and tribute for its own sake. There was a skirmish, and the one pantheon became two. The gods In'zdul borrows magic from are what my mother called the Dark Pantheon, those who demand sacrifice and enforce servitude in exchange for the erasure of a normal moral code.

Anyway, enough of ancient history. In'zdul might indeed use magic to keep his crimes secret. I was horrified to think of Zeeim's mother dying for In'zdul's purposes, but it seemed likely.

"I really want to eat this guy," I told Dibbins.

"Don't," he said. "He would probably make you sick." I laughed for a moment, and so did Dibbins. Then we both became morose again.

"Tell me about his other crimes, Dibbins," I said. "He's going to die if I have anything to say about it. I want to know all that he's going to die for."

"I don't know much more," Dibbins said. "My father might, I guess."

"Then can we go see him?"

"Of course—we have to anyway, after all," Dibbins said.

"We do?"

"To deliver my half of the treasure."

"Oh, right," I said. I suddenly remembered what Dibbins had said about his father accepting the conquering of his kingdom. "I thought your father didn't want to fight," I said.

"He doesn't. Father hates war. He just hates black magic more." Dibbins said.

"Good." I replied. "Well, I'm too tired to fly straight. We'll leave in the morning. Good night, Dibbins."

"Good night."

I held onto Zeeim, and drifted off to sleep, hoping not to have any more nightmares.

I woke up because Zeeim was bouncing on me. That's right, he was bouncing. On *me*. I was less than pleased.

"Get up! Get up!" He squealed.

I groaned. "Is something wrong?"

"No.

"Get up!" I sat up slowly, wondering if adopting Zeeim had been such a good choice after all (don't worry, I'm kidding.) Zeeim slid off me and bounced over to Dibbins, who had built a fire and was roasting some kind of meat over it. Zeeim sniffed gingerly at it, then sneezed and hopped back, looking disgusted.

"Look, Zeeim," I said, pointing, "there's a patch of nice grass right there. Go get your breakfast." He scooted away and settled down on his stomach to eat. I turned to Dibbins.

"So we're going to see your father today?"

"Yes," he said.

"And he'll be okay with a visiting dragon?"

"Lethina takes a better attitude toward dragons than most human civilizations. Although it's probably good that only one dragon come in. I don't think my father would be very happy to see a whole army of dragons arrive."

What with one thing and another (things like gathering more clover for Zeeim, and Dibbins stopping to sew up a hole in his magic bag) it took us a couple of hours before we were ready to go. Finally we got into the air, though, and Dibbins called out directions to me.

"The other left!" He said for the third time.

"Well don't blame me, dragons don't use 'right' and 'left'! You're just lucky I know what they are!"

"What do you use, then?" Dibbins hollered.

"Three hundred and twenty-two different directions, going in all the ways a sphere does, oriented by the angle of the sun."

"Oh. I think I'll stick with left and right," he said.

"I thought you would. Is that your kingdom up ahead?" I felt Dibbins lean to the side a little to see what I was looking at.

"Yes, that's Lethina!"

Dibbins told me to land in front of the palace gates so as to make a grand entrance. In honor of the occasion, I made my scales white, tinged gold at the tips to match the palace. We landed in front of the monumental building, the sun shining down from its near-noon position.

[Fig. 7, Palace Lethina]

The guard in front of the gate turned very white when he saw me.

Good.

Dibbins raised both hands in the air.

"Hello, Ettim!"

"Prince Arrik?"

"Yes, Ettim. I told you I'd come back safely. Send word to my father immediately, we need an audience with him. In the next five minutes. Go." The still-pale guard raised both hands in a salute, then turned around and ran into the palace.

CHAPTER SIX

The King's chamber for receiving formal audiences was built to comfortably admit about ten people. Fifteen if they were all exceptionally thin. It was not built for a dragon.

Which just goes to show how rude humans can be. Any dragon would have space for visiting people! They ought to show the same courtesy.

You're interrupting again. Right in the middle of my rant, too, which further shows the rude nature of human beings. I'm miffed. Yes, I heard what you said. The fact that dragons generally have more space has nothing to do with it. It was impolite of the king not to have enough space for me.

Not that he wasn't hospitable otherwise. He soon had us shown into his great dining hall instead, which *was* big enough for me. He even had a stack of vegetables brought in for Zeeim.

I think he would have fed me too, but humans have this silly idea that dragons only eat princesses. Dibbins apologized for his father's lack of understanding. Zeeim dug into the vegetables (I mean that literally. He started digging in the heap like it was dirt and he was building a tunnel. I didn't feel like telling him not to play with his food.) Dibbins and I didn't even sit down; we just waited for the king. It only took him a few minutes to arrive, which I appreciated—spatially accommodating he might not have been, but he was politely punctual.

King Roberr was one of those folks that shout everything they say when they're nervous or excited (I have an uncle like that.) He slammed the door open, boomed out a greeting to his son (I actually took a moment to realize who he was addressing when he said, "ARRIK!"), and threw out a hand for me to shake with a bellow of,

"NICE TO MEET YOU, MISTER DRAGON! I AM KING ROBERR OF LETHINA." Dibbins whispered to his father, who flushed. "MISS DRAGON. I APOLOGIZE,

LITTLE MISTAKE, I DON'T HAVE A LOT OF PRACTICE

TELLING THE DIFFERENCE, YOU KNOW. HOPE YOU'LL

FORGIVE THAT LITTLE SLIP OF THE TONGUE!"

"Um, yes, sir," I said. The hall's acoustics echoed

everything the King said until my earholes hurt. "Not a

problem," I added, though I was fighting not to blush. I don't

think I look masculine. But I was trying to be polite for Dibbins'

sake.

"Father," Dibbins said, "this is the dragon Izznae of the

volcano Spendidium. She's been a great help to me personally

and to our nation, and we owe her our gratitude."

"Splendid, lad, splendid!" The King said. He didn't roar

it the way he had done previously, but he wasn't exactly

whispering either. "Well, Izznae, how can the kingdom of

Lethina help you today?" I turned to Dibbins.

"Dibbins, could we send Zeeim into another room?"

"Sure," Dibbins said at the same time his father called out, "'*Dibbins*'?" The Dibbins in question snapped his fingers and a guard came and scooped up Zeeim and his vegetables.

"Mamma!" He squealed, scratching at the guard.

"Relax, Zeeim," I said. "He's going to take you…" I trailed off in confusion, looking to the guard for help.

"The royal warren, ma'am," he said.

"He's going to take you to play with some other rabbits, Zeeim!" Zeeim relaxed and returned to munching on the cabbage he had laid siege to. After the door swung closed behind him and the guard, I turned back to the king.

"I apologize for my charge, your majesty," I said. "He's more nervous than your average rabbit."

"WELL, THAT'S SAYING SOMETHING!" King Roberr boomed dismissively. "Do sit down; we need to discuss business. Arrik wouldn't have brought you here without a good reason, would you, my boy?"

It's funny how the groaning of an entire volcano (yeah, they groan. Especially when the sun rises early; I think Spendidium likes to sleep in) doesn't bother me at all, but King Roberr's volume really put a strain on me. I was starting to wince just a little every time he spoke. Thankfully, Dibbins cut in with what I was just starting to appreciate as his quiet way.

He explained to his father about meeting me and about the dwarves. I half-listened, wondering at the same time what kind of rocks this kingdom had to offer (I was hungry again,) until Dibbins jerked me out of my reverie by saying something that surprised me.

"I think we've seen evidence that In'zdul is using a new branch of black magic, Father."

We had? I thought about it. I mean, we hadn't even met the guy. Enchantment on the treasure—nope, that wasn't even black magic. Killing Zeeim's mother—nope, Dibbins had already known about that. The magic the dwarves used on me—

nope, that was black in *my* opinion certainly, but any curse that wore off so soon was not classified as evil.

"YOU HAVE?" King Roberr exclaimed, coming halfway out of his chair in surprise and—I thought—fear. "What kind?"

"I think," Dibbins said slowly, "that he is altering the nature of sentient creatures. I assume to enslave them."

I blinked at Dibbins—not that he noticed, my eyelids were clear at the time. Where was he getting this? If it was true, In'zdul had sunk into some of the worst magic known. It's a branch so terrible that it has its own name: *"Kiteweyn."* Translated from the original Unirun (Unicorn language) it means roughly "soul destruction."

You want to know what makes it so evil? Alright, I'll tell you.

All intelligent creatures in Daiines share some fundamental beliefs, although there are several facets of religion. We all believe in the gods, both good and despicable. We all believe in our ability to do right and go to the happy afterlife—dragons call it "Nittimaan." The creatures of this world also believe in an unhappy life that the gods must send us to if we commit terrible deeds. (I'd tell you what we call it, but my mother told me not to use that word.)

There is another belief, though, that all intelligent beings on our planet share. We believe that when the first god, who gave the other gods their mission of watching over the world, made the world, he did it with exact intentions. More specifically, we all believe that he created all creatures with fundamental qualities that are not to be changed.

The gods are often merciful and forgiving, and accidental transgressions do not have to keep us out of Nittimaan. But to sin against the original laws takes effort. To do so, one must turn away from all the goodness in his soul. The practice of Kiteweyn is doing something which breaks one of the few laws that the original god left us. In In'zdul's case, if what Dibbins said was true, he was breaking the law against changing the fundamental nature of creatures. And then to add a magical slavery on top of it… I was very glad not to have to face the gods in In'zdul's place.

However, I was still not convinced that Dibbins had evidence of In'zdul practicing Kiteweyn. I mean, *I* hadn't seen any, or not that I could think of. I thought maybe Dibbins just hated the guy (I sure did) and wanted to encourage his father to bring In'zdul down.

"What proof have you, my boy?" For a moment I thought someone other than King Roberr was speaking; he had all but whispered. I didn't even know he could do that. He was definitely scared—and I didn't blame him.

"What do you know about the nature of rabbits?" Dibbins asked.

Rabbits?

King Roberr seemed as confused as I was. At last he answered (still mercifully in a normal tone of voice,)

"They are very *good*. More than many creatures. But to balance out that great gift, they are shy. Very shy. And afraid much more than other creatures."

"That's all true," Dibbins said to his father, "what do you know about their intelligence?"

"Intelligence?" As King Roberr recovered from the shock of In'zdul's supposed crimes, he had gotten loud again. Fire scorch it! (I believe humans are known for saying "blast" in such situations.) "I believe that among their own people there are those of great cleverness. And they're said to be wise. But they are not known among other peoples as great thinkers, learners, or teachers. That's why we sometimes forget that they are even one of the intelligent species." I shot a glare at Dibbins at that; I hadn't forgotten his, "mumble, something, yadda, stew," from the morning we met Zeeim.

Zeeim.

"Zeeim?" I gasped. Dibbins nodded at me.

"Think about it, Iz," he said. "Have you ever heard of a rabbit picking up languages the way Zeeim does? And he understands other things fast, too. I first noticed it when he freed me from the ropes that the dwarves had tied me with. Zeeim looked over the knots and cut me free in a single bite. I'd thought when they tied me up that the knots were complicated; I'd have had to cut the rope in about ten places to free myself. Zeeim saw a smarter way to do it." I nodded thoughtfully. Dibbins had been awfully trussed before Zeeim chomped him free. "And he knew somehow that In'zdul was the one who burned his mother. I somehow doubt that he could have known that if he hadn't met In'zdul. He's really no more than a baby, Iz. I'm willing to bet that he's smarter than any other rabbit his age—unless In'zdul enchanted more."

"I can see why In'zdul thought it was a good plan," I mused. "Enchant rabbits so that they're brilliant—never mind the awful rites involved—and you don't even have to put a lot of magical effort into turning them into slaves. They're rabbits. They're easily cowed." (Which makes you wonder why the word is "cowed" and not "rabbitted," doesn't it? Just a thought.) King Roberr was nodding.

"But why start making slaves now? Why mess around with Kiteweyn now?" Oh, blessed day. I was starting to think that I could get along with King Roberr just fine if I could keep him frightened enough to stop shouting.

"What about as practice for something bigger?" Dibbins asked.

"Like what?" I asked.

"Well, rabbits are small and probably easier to use Kiteweyn on than some creatures—they don't have the same strength of will that some species do. Like humans, for instance."

"Humans?" King Roberr and I asked at the same time.

"Think about it, Father," Dibbins continued in something of a bitter tone. "You said yourself that it seemed strange to have the kingdom of Carobinn attack us now, after centuries of peace. They lost a fortune in trade by fighting us as well. Why would they do that?"

"You mean," I said as I began to see where Dibbins was going, "you think In'zdul used Kiteweyn on the king of Carobinn?"

"Queen." King Roberr grunted.

"What?"

"Carobinn is ruled by a queen," King Roberr said.

"Oh," I said, not seeing why that should be relevant. Human is human. "But Dibbins, you think the war with

Carobinn is coming from an enchantment? You think In'zdul is causing it? Why would he bother?"

"I suspect he wants to rule the world," King Roberr mused. "Isn't that always the goal of villains and madmen? And In'zdul is certainly both. Carobinn is close to Coortain, where In'zdul lives. He would have little trouble getting there to enchant Queen Hazebbul. So now he's using it to conquer the surrounding nations, starting with us because we are the smallest." King Roberr shook his head. "You were right, Arrik," he said to his son, "we should have kept fighting Carobinn."

"You've stopped?" I asked, shocked.

"Nearly," the King admitted. He sighed, slouching a little into an old man's stance. "Well, what else could I do?" He asked indignantly. "I have almost no soldiers—most of the inhabitants of Lethina are farmers. And we have no more money for mercenaries."

"Um," I said.

"Um," Dibbins said. We looked at each other and both burst out in laughter, shattering the tension that was so heavy in the room.

"I told you my adventure was a good idea, Father," Dibbins said, and pulled the cord on the treasure bag nearest him. Gems and coins cascaded down my back and bounced across the floor—I gritted my teeth and tried not to whimper at this terrible mistreatment of valuables. Dibbins walked around, pulling the other cords loose so that the artifacts and magic articles and strings of precious and semi-precious stones and even the strange paper money of the kingdoms to the far north fell to the floor in a concerto of clatters. As his father stared, Dibbins helped me get the bags off of my back (they were starting to be uncomfortable.) While his father stared, he made the guard (who was already well trained) swear not to tell even his wife about the mound of wealth on the floor of the great dining hall. Honestly, while his father stared I think I could have written this whole book.

Eventually King Roberr raised his head, his jaw still hanging open (an admirably dragon-like quality.) A moment later he closed his mouth and forced his expression into one of complete calm.

"Guh." The King managed to say.

Dibbins just grinned.

CHAPTER SEVEN

"Iz, you're the best. The absolute best. Really." Dibbins said.

It's like he thought I didn't know that already or something.

"WE THANK YOU MOST COMPLETELY, DRAGON IZZNAE," King Roberr said. Personally I thought it might have been more appropriate for him to say he thanked me most *THUNDEROUSLY,* but I kept it to myself. I nodded as graciously as any dragon could to a human.

"I owe it to Zeeim to see this out, your majesty. In'zdul had no right to change him the way he did."

In the four days since Dibbins and I had shown King Roberr his treasure—his half of the treasure, as I had carefully divided it out with the bellowing king—he had gotten to work very quickly. Under his direction, the Duke of the Treasury had decided which treasures could be spent to pay the soldiers, the Duke of War had hired mercenaries, the Duke of Magic had analyzed Zeeim (much to Zeeim's annoyance) and decided that Dibbins was right and In'zdul had used Kiteweyn on Zeeim, and the Duke of Cooking had made meals for all of us. Even me. I was enticed to try several human foods, most of which were completely wretched. I liked the stale bread, though, even if its texture was a bit soft. Potato chips also appealed to me as they crunched through my teeth.

And, as his cabinet took care of other tasks, the king sat with Dibbins and me and planned. On the third day he leaned back in his chair, stretched, and roared,

"WELL, I THINK THERE'S NO HELP FOR IT, ARRIK. I THINK YOU WILL HAVE TO GO VISIT QUEEN HAZEBBUL AND GET THE ENCHANTMENT OFF HER. YOU'LL HAVE TO SNEAK IN, THOUGH." Personally I couldn't see the point of sneaking when King Roberr's voice had probably carried all the way back to Spendidium, but I supposed he was right. So I volunteered to be Dibbins' ride to Carobinn.

Yeah, I know it wasn't the smartest thing to do. But Dibbins had sort of grown on me, and I wanted to finish out our adventure. Plus I might have been a little bit of the smallest amount worried about what my parents would say when I got back. But, you know, only a little.

So we packed up—food for Dibbins and Zeeim (who was, of course, coming along,) and a properly "safe" sling for Zeeim to ride in, and all of the instruments we needed to lift the enchantment from off Queen Hazebbul. I wasn't entirely thrilled at having such a heavy load to bring along, but it was hardly beyond what I could carry.

Still a dragon. In case you'd forgotten.

Zeeim was the sad one among us. Dibbins and I were excited, ready to go knock down the evil sorcerer dwarf. Zeeim, however, had enjoyed the sweet (in his opinion. Blegh.) vegetables and the company of other rabbits. Particularly he enjoyed a lovely chocolate-colored female. I had to promise him more than once that we would come back before he consented to go.

Zeeim's speech had improved considerably in just a few days. His caretakers used him as an interpreter between them and the other rabbits, and he had picked up a good deal more Dracogin as well. Dibbins and I had wondered, at first, whether the Duke of Magic might change Zeeim back, but he declined. Actually, he started shuddering and told us that to return Zeeim to his original state would require the use of Kiteweyn again, something the Duke would not do and we would not allow. So Zeeim was stuck being the world's smartest rabbit (something which, evidently, did not bother his female friend.)

The dawn of the fifth day after we arrived in Lethina was, unfortunately, something I witnessed. Not unlike the volcano I call home, I dislike the early morning. I made a sound something like,

"Egmppathnggggrtnn."

I wouldn't have woken up at all, but the stupid attendants actually *heralded* when Dibbins—their beloved Prince Arrik—came to knock on my door. I made a note to eat them at a more reasonable time, then called out to Dibbins to enter.

"Come on, Iz," he said, "time for you to get up."

I thought about eating him, too. Then I grumbled a little, stretched, and sat up—at which point I hit my head on the ceiling. Ow. What a terrible way to start the day.

Eventually we got everything loaded and strapped down on my back, Zeeim in his sling, and Dibbins straddling my krane in his usual space.

"No offense, Iz," he groaned, "but you're really uncomfortable." Just for that I took off a lot faster and steeper than was actually necessary.

Hey—I didn't throw him off!

The flight wasn't all that bad. The currents were with us most of the time, so I got to glide a lot rather than flapping. I did my best to ignore the troops of soldiers marching beneath me, and Dibbins avoided mentioning them. He spread a map out in front of him and called out directions to me. Finally, as the sun began to set, I saw the capital city of Carobinn (humans have a habit of naming their capitals the same thing they name their countries.) It wasn't as neat as Lethina; it kind of sprawled out in all directions, and the entire place was a mass of steep hills and deep valleys, with a lake flung from outside the city boundaries clear to the middle of the place. I liked it. The rigidity of Lethina had made me uncomfortable; it was all right angles and completely flat and boring.

"Iz, aim for that peninsula closer to us," Dibbins shouted over the wind. I spiraled down through the evening sky, breathing in the scent of the rocks of Carobinn. Yup. I liked that place.

An arrow flew past me.

Now, let's remember, I'm a dragon. Have I mentioned that? So I knew the arrow wouldn't have hurt me even if it had hit. But the fact that someone had the audacity to shoot at me made me really, *really* annoyed.

A tip? Don't annoy a dragon.

I dropped, plunging toward the place the arrow had come from. Zeeim was safely entangled in his sling below me, but Dibbins grabbed the aught in front of him and hollered like the world was ending. I landed in front of a terrified-looking man in what I guessed was a soldier's uniform (although honestly I have a bit of trouble telling the difference between one piece of human clothing and any other,) clinging with trembling hands to a crossbow.

I love when they tremble.

Remember how my parents were all excited when I was born because they knew I was going to be a great fire-breather? Well, I took all that firepower and rage and blasted a column of flame into the sky. An entire cloud dissipated where my fire roared through it, re-forming higher up. I kept burning the sky until Dibbins screamed over the crackling, roaring noise that he was overheating. I turned my head to look at him; he had sweat pouring off every part of him (oh, how I love to be a dragon) and his hair was singed in front.

[Fig. 8, Izznae Breathing Fire]

"Sorry," I said, smoke rushing out of my mouth. I turned back to the soldier.

"What's your name?" I demanded of the guard.

"S-S-Stephann."

"Well, Stephann, tell the rest of your army. The next person who tries to hurt me or my friends gets charred." Stephann, also sweating, saluted me, then ran away.

"Um, Iz?" Dibbins said. I looked back at him again.

"What?" Breathing so much fire made me a little testy.

"I didn't realize you could do that. I'm glad Zeeim didn't see it." I nodded, suddenly too tired to say much. Even with my incredible natural talent, breathing out a firestorm like the one I had just created was exhausting.

I took a nap.

When I woke up, Dibbins and Zeeim were playing some version of tag, racing up and down the hill to the left of us underneath the bright rising moon. I stretched, then called out to the runaways,

"You ready to go?"

"Nope. I'm winning," Zeeim said. I laughed.

"One more round, Zeeim, and then we need to go."

It didn't take long at all to arrive on the back lawn of Queen Hazebbul's palace. I turned myself the color of the grass at midnight and Dibbins slunk along behind me, hiding.

"Where to?" I whispered.

"Second floor, third window from the left," Dibbins hissed back. I paused a moment, wondering how Dibbins knew that. Dibbins stepped on my camouflaged krane. Ugh.

We stole across the rest of the lawn and over a short wall. Dibbins climbed up onto my back and I sunk my fiings into the palace wall, pulling us both up to the Queen's window. Dibbins opened it—slowly, without the least consideration for me, suffering, clinging to the wall by my fiings—and climbed inside. Luckily, the window was massive, and I squeezed through too. It was uncomfortable though.

Again, humans lack courtesy.

Oh. Well I guess that's true, they weren't really expecting a dragon to break in.

The ceiling was too low, of course. Zeeim climbed out of his sling, rather than having me squat on his head. After I made sure both he and the top of my head were safe from the danger of squishing, I looked around. Dibbins was standing next to a large, canopied bed; he reached out and gently touched the one occupant.

"Haze," he said softly to the sleeper, "Hazebbul, wake up."

The sleeping Queen sat up so fast I thought she might pull a muscle. I caught sight of her terrified eyes before Dibbins clapped a hand over her mouth. He guided her head so that she could see him. When she did, her body lost its sharp tension. Dibbins slowly pulled his hand off her face.

"Arrik?" She said strangely sleepily. "Oh. I'm dreaming again."

"No," Dibbins said. He sat down on the edge of the bed. "Haze, I'm really here." He reached out and laid a hand on top of one of hers. "You can feel me. I'm real."

"No," she said, "no, I'm dreaming. Or else… you're here to kidnap me?" She tensed again, and Dibbins' hand returned to cover her mouth.

"Queen Hazebbul," he said, sounding more like a prince than I had ever heard, "Relax. Have peace. We're not here to hurt you." She stared at him for a moment, then pulled his hand away from her face.

"We?" Dibbins pointed to me. Wisely, Queen Hazebbul didn't scream when she saw me. In fact, she looked completely unsurprised.

"I haven't dreamed of dragons since I was a child," she said. Her tone had changed; where a moment before she had sounded queenly, she now sounded very small, as if she were that child again. Then her eyes grew wide, and she turned back to Dibbins.

"Arrik—I have only a moment—the war—" she froze. Dibbins and I exchanged a look while Queen Hazebbul sat unmoving. Seriously, she went statue on us. It was freaky. Then, as if she had no idea anyone else was in the room, she pulled her covers back up and laid down to sleep again.

"So..." I said awkwardly.

"So now we break the spell?" Dibbins said. I nodded, thinking.

"Dibbins, I think she's breaking through it herself. She had that moment of clarity."

"Of course she is," Dibbins said, "she's strong." He looked at her fondly, and tucked her blanket more closely around her.

"Dibbins, are you two…"

"Betrothed." He said shortly. Then he paused, and added, "and in love. That's part of why I couldn't fathom Carobinn just declaring war on Lethina. Even if it had made sense politically, which it doesn't, Haze wouldn't—" he stopped abruptly.

"I'm sorry Dibbins," I said.

"It's not your fault, Iz. Besides, you've gone way out of your way to help me."

"You're right," I said, "it's not my fault. It's In'zdul's." Dibbins nodded, a nasty expression on his face. "Well," I said, "if you want, *you* can eat him instead of me doing it." Dibbins looked at me in shock for a moment, then realized I was kidding. We laughed so hard and so loud that Queen Hazebbul's guards came in. They stopped short when they saw me.

"Good night, gentlemen," Dibbins said.

"Prince Arrik?" asked the guard in the silliest hat. "What are you doing here? In Carobinn, not the Queen's room. Although, what are you doing in the Queen's room? And why is there a dragon with you? Or are you a prisoner of the dragon? Why don't you answer me? Are you under some spell?" I snorted; how could Dibbins possibly answer, with the questions coming so fast? I started listening again when the guard asked, "And why, in the name of dryads and drag—um, er, just—*why* is a rabbit snuggled up against my boot?"

"Zeeim?" I asked; I hadn't noticed that he was nuzzling the guard's leg.

"I was just trying to make him feel better."

"It's very nice of you to try," I told him gently, "but I'm afraid he might kick you by accident." Zeeim hopped immediately back to my side.

The guard was staring at me.

"Yes?" I asked.

"You're... well, you're a dragon."

"Yes."

"And I'm not dreaming?"

"I'm afraid not." The guard turned to one of his comrades.

"Run and tell the doctor to stop bleeding Stephann; it seems that he wasn't delusional after all." He snapped. A soldier nodded and backed out of the room, staring at me.

"Are you here to kidnap the Queen?" The chief soldier asked.

"No," I said, rolling my eyes as if to say, What would a dragon want with a Queen?

"Oh good. Just checking. Have a good night then, ma'am."

Being called "ma'am" was almost as annoying as being called "sir" by accident, but I let the guards scurry out like frightened mice anyway. I guess that soldier, Stephann, had gotten the word about my threat around.

"So," I said to Dibbins, "let's see about lifting this enchantment."

CHAPTER EIGHT

Love does funny things to people—not just human people, all kinds of people. Dragons do funny things for love, mostly pulling incredibly dangerous stunts to catch each other's attention (it's amazing we reproduce at all, really,) and then later weird things like building giant nests and using explosive magic to celebrate the joy of their lives. Rabbits get infected by love too, staying with their mates as much as they possibly can (it is not nearly so surprising that rabbits reproduce.) Unicorns perform tricks (like balancing on their horns. I saw that once, after the events of this tale, and it was awesome,) and feats of incredible strength. Centaurs go on long journeys with their spouses shortly after they are bound to one another, sometimes not returning for years. Bears dig massive home caves and line them with feathers (yes, I heard you, and no, I don't care that animals behave differently where you're from; you're from not here, so it's not important.) Butterflies dance together for hours on end. And humans get this crazy protective instinct that makes them willing to do just about anything to keep those they love from harm.

So it's not all that surprising, really, that Dibbins decided to kidnap Queen Hazebbul.

Well, I guess *kidnap* isn't the word. Really we just sort of *borrowed* her. I even had Dibbins leave a note for the guard, explaining. He seemed like a nice fellow, after all, and it seemed a shame for him to have his head cut off for something that was actually going to help the kingdom.

But, whether she was kidnapped or borrowed or went on vacation without knowing it, she was lifted out of her window as the moon reached its zenith. Dibbins eased her onto my back as she continued to snooze in what could only have been an enchanted sleep.

Not the good kind of enchantment, by the way.

Now, Dibbins and I didn't filch the Queen for nothing. The Duke of Magic had given us very detailed instructions (including diagrams!) about how to lift the enchantment on the Queen. It couldn't be performed in the Queen's bedchamber or, indeed, anywhere near the palace.

Magic is even trickier than love, I think.

We—I— hauled the purloined, sleeping Queen to the top of a hill that was shrouded in willow trees. I had thought that finding such a place would take *ages*, that we might not even get there in time for the dawn we needed for the magic, but thankfully Dibbins had spent a fair amount of time in Carobinn and knew the perfect place to go. He seemed a little sad when I landed atop the hill, like it brought back difficult memories for him. I wondered if the place held some significance for him and the queen.

"Dibbins, does this place have some kind of significance for you and the queen? You seem a little sad." Subtlety is not one of my many gifts.

Dibbins cocked his head, looking at me.

"You know," he said, "I never thought I'd tell a dragon about any of this. But I trust you, Iz."

"Good. Keeping secrets *is* one of my many gifts."
Dibbins laid a hand against the trunk of a tree thoughtfully.

"Yes, this place means something to me. To both of us." He nodded at the Queen's sleeping form. "We both grew up knowing that one day we would be married. We had no real knowledge of one another though; each of us was required to focus entirely on our studies of running a kingdom and the responsibilities that come with it. Still, we weren't even allowed to write to one another—I suppose our parents thought that we might become distracted from the things we were supposed to be learning.

"I ached with curiosity though. I used to ask my tutors what she looked like, what her favorite color was, if she was funny…" Dibbins broke off, smiling at some faded memory. "Then, when I turned seventeen, my parents told me that we would travel to Carobinn and I would meet my future bride. I remember I was so nervous that I sweated through all my layers of clothes and even into the saddle of my horse. They had to provide me with different clothes before we arrived, and I had to change in a thicket." I thought this was a testament to the superiority of dragons—no sweat, no clothing, no having to change among briars. "And when I arrived, I found that she had run away! She was afraid that if she met me she wouldn't like me. So she dashed off, dressed up though she was. I was excused from my parents' counsels with Haze's parents. I was supposed to wait in my chamber in the palace, but I didn't want to; I was restless.

"So instead I went walking. I must have walked for at least an hour before I saw this hill and decided to climb it. The sun had started setting, and I thought I might like seeing the kingdom from the hilltop in the rosy light. And when I got to the top, she was there. She sat with her back against one of the trees, watching the sun fade into the horizon. I knew who she was from the moment I saw her. And I knew then that she was exactly what I had always secretly hoped she was. She wasn't just beautiful, I could see that she was strong, and wise, and kind, and intelligent, and loved to laugh." Dibbins stopped, lost in some secret train of thought.

"So what happened?" I asked when I felt he needed prompting.

"The palace guards found us the next morning, still sitting under the trees. We had talked until dawn without even being aware of the time. And by then we knew that our marriage would be one not only of convenience, but of love and joy as well."

"But aren't you both old enough to marry?" I asked. I couldn't understand what had taken them so long if they both wanted to be together. "Why haven't you gotten around to it yet?"

"Politics," Dibbins said, "and bad luck. We told our parents that we wanted to be married as fast as it could be arranged—which, for a royal wedding, meant about three years of waiting anyway. We wrote to one another, visited as often as we could. But then a plague swept through her kingdom and killed her mother. The wedding was put on hold so that the royal family of Carobinn and its people could mourn. Haze came here to grieve, and this is where I found her and held her while she wept. It's our place."

"But you're still not married," I said. "Why not?"

Dibbins sighed.

"Because her father was killed a year or so later by centaurs. There's an uncomfortable truce between the centaurs and Carobinn, and the king was holding peace talks with them. A rogue who didn't want his people to make peace with the humans assassinated the king." Dibbins sounded bitter. "So Princess Hazebbul became Queen Hazebbul of Carobinn, and she's been struggling to gain control of her kingdom since then. The people love her, but they only really started to respect her as an adequate ruler recently—she was so young when she took the throne, it worried them. Then, just when I thought that things were settling down and we could finally marry, In'zdul came along and started this war between our countries."

"I'm sorry, Dibbins," I said.

"It's still not your fault, Iz," he said.

"I'm still sorry for you. But we'll lift this enchantment and stop the war and you will invite me to the wedding."

"Sure thing, Iz," Dibbins said, and a grin found its way across his face.

We set up the hill in accordance with the diagrams, placing the queen between a great marble basin of water and a carefully constructed campfire. Dibbins donned the scarlet robes of a mage, and I scraped a circle (do you have any idea how hard it is to make a perfect circle?) into the dirt around him and Queen Hazebbul. Then we sat and waited for hours.

It was the most boring part of our whole adventure. Even inside the dwarves' cave we were nervous enough to feel active. Dibbins was lost in thought and Zeeim was asleep, so I sat with my krane wrapped around a tree. I tried not to think about my parents, and about Mooninga, who would be worried about me. I tried not to think about how much I missed them. I tried not to think about the roasting trouble I would be in when I got home. But I guess I didn't try hard enough.

"Dibbins," I asked just as the stars began to fade, a hopeful sign of oncoming dawn. "Do you have any siblings?"

He looked at me, his eyebrows raised (which made him look silly. Eyebrows. Pfft.)

"Yes, Iz, I do. I'm not even the oldest in my family."

"Wait, then you're not going to take over ruling Lethina?"

"No, that will be my older brother," he said.

"But I thought you said you spent, like, your entire childhood studying how to run a kingdom."

"I did," he said, a touch of laughter in his voice, "but not my own. Haze and I were betrothed just after she was born, when I was only three. I've been prepared ever since then to be King of Carobinn."

"Huh." I said. I understood why that made sense, but it was still weird in my mind.

"And I have two younger siblings," he continued, "they're twins, a boy and a girl. And there's another brother sort of."

"Sort of?"

"Well, he's not my actual brother. Larrite is my cousin, and he spent his early years right here in Carobinn. But his parents were killed by the same plague that killed Haze's mother, and he's lived with my family ever since. We count him as one of us now, even though he's the youngest by many years."

"Interesting," I said. It was a properly dragonish thing to do, taking in your orphaned cousin. Dragons have a policy that no one—from the newest draclet to the oldest droog (the name given to those who are teetering on the edge of their rest in the lava)—will ever be denied a family. There wasn't a lot of difficulty with that in Spendidium, since no knights came to slaughter us there, but there were chapters in the general dragon history that involved taking in a lot of orphaned refugees.

Musing, I thought that this was probably why I had adopted

Zeeim; it was against my nature to leave him to struggle alone.

"Iz?" Dibbins asked, yanking me out of my thoughts.

"Yeah?"

"Why do you ask? About my family, I mean."

"Oh." For a moment I considered throwing out some

plausible excuse. But Dibbins had told me his secrets, and it

seemed just that I should tell him mine as well—not that it was

really a secret. "I was just thinking about my little sister,

Mooninga. She and I are tight. Super tight. She's my best

friend—my only friend, really."

"What?" Dibbins interrupted. "What do you mean?" I

sighed slowly.

"I'm not especially… well-liked at home. I mean, my

parents love me, and Mooninga loves me…" I trailed off. I

glanced at Dibbins out of the corner of my eye; he was watching me, focused on what I was saying. If he had looked at me in pity

or annoyance I probably would have told him that it wasn't his

business, anyway, and changed the subject. But he was looking

at me with curiosity and understanding. And Dibbins had never

treated me with scorn; he had treated me like his friend. So I

kept talking. It was hard, saying things out loud that I'd only

ever thought privately before.

"The truth is, even my parents think I'm weird, despite

all their love. Mooninga is the closest to understanding me, but

even she doesn't fully understand the fixation."

"Huh?" Dibbins asked.

"All dragons like treasure. That's normal. But all my life

I've been completely obsessed, putting the quest for ownership

before everything else. I'm probably the best fire-breather my

age in Spendidium, but I never cared. Fire bored me. The games

the other dragons my age played seemed trite and dull. They

thought my absolute adoration of treasure was freakish, and so they ignored me. And I ignored them. Nobody really talked to me after they realized how much I didn't fit in. When Mooninga was hatched, I was afraid she would be like all the rest of them and think I was a fanatic and a weirdo. And then she started growing up, and it was so incredible to have a friend. She fit in with the other dragons, and she got some of them to tolerate me, stopped some of the bullies."

"It sounds like she's done a lot of good for you," Dibbins said.

"Yeah." I paused. "And after all of that, I ran off on an adventure without her. Dibbins, I'm afraid." I choked on the last word. I felt like I had finally lost everything that made me a proper dragon.

"Of what?"

I looked at him again. He looked like he sincerely meant the question. He wasn't mocking, he wasn't pitying, he wasn't shocked that even a dragon can feel fear.

"I'm afraid she'll be mad at me." Dibbins reached out and patted my foreleg.

"Well Iz, if she is, I bet she will forgive you. And you know what?"

"What?" I whispered it, feeling like I was choking over my words.

"I bet more than anything she will just be glad to have you home."

"Thanks, Dibbins," I said. The stars were all gone from the sky now, and the black of night was fading into a pale blue streaked with orange and gold. I swallowed all the emotions rising inside me, then turned to him. "Now let's go un-enchant your queen." Dibbins smiled and picked up the instructions for the spell. I turned and headed toward my spot, hoping that the Duke of Magic knew what he was doing. Dibbins called my name and I looked back at him.

"Mooninga's not your only friend anymore, Iz. You've got me." I smiled at Dibbins.

"Yeah, Dibbins, you've got me too."

Gross. Emotional moments are the worst.

CHAPTER NINE

The Duke of Magic, it turned out, was pretty good at his job. We laid the queen down in the center of the circle. I donated a scale that was about to fall off anyway, and that was the end of my role in the magic. I had to sit outside the circle while Dibbins used Zeeim to take the spell off of Hazebbul. Totally boring.

Dibbins dipped the scale into the water, pouring it over Zeeim. Zeeim shivered and snapped at Dibbins even though he had known what was coming. Dibbins allowed the water to drip off Zeeim into the fire, where it raised a cloud of plum-colored steam that smelled like nastiness. Zeeim shuddered and tried to snuggle against Dibbins, but Dibbins set him down. Zeeim charged out of the circle to sit by me (I'm naturally warm. Dragon.)

Dibbins poured more water from my generously given scale over Hazebbul, who continued to sleep. Dibbins lifted her up and carried her so that the water from her also dripped on the fire (which charred her hair a bit as well. Oops.) The same wretched-smelling dark purple steam rose from the fire, showing us that both Hazebbul and Zeeim were enchanted by the same corrupted magician. Dibbins returned Hazebbul's body to the grass in the center of the circle and reached into a pouch on his sorcerer's robes, pulling out a powder that smelled so strongly sweet that I gagged where I was. He poured it over the Queen, then stopped and consulted the Duke of Magic's step-by-step instructions. In the light of the dawn I could see that he was crying a little. I watched in fascination as he stood, his hand held out in front of him, and started to speak. As he did the wind picked up around him so that he had to shout so I could hear his words:

Turn of wind and kiss of moon,

Song of breeze through grasses,

Draw from this the blessed one

The soul safe, unenchanted.

He continued the spell with different powders and liquids, chanting in Human, Dragogin, and Unirun (the original language of magic,) occasionally stopping to lay a hand on the Queen's face. Finally he laid down his magicky stuff and lifted the Queen into his arms.

By flame a'charmed and night bright lit,

By touch of ancient magic,

Untie this cursed warlock's knot

And find thyself, unaltered.

For the space of two breaths the only thing that changed was that the wind died down. In that perfect silence I feared that Queen Hazebbul had died, that Dibbins had just made the war much worse for his people. And then I saw that a faint purple mist was rising off the Queen's body. It became denser and deeper until at last she was completely obscured from my view.

"Dibbins?" I asked tentatively. "What do we do?" He was searching the instructions frantically.

"There was a—footnote—about this…" he trailed off, squinting at the page. Then a look of horror came over him, followed by an expression of determination. "It's In'zdul fighting back against our magic, Iz. He placed a counterspell in her. You have to roast her. Dragon fire can burn off some kinds of magic."

"What?" I asked.

"Now! Iz, breathe fire at her. NOW, IZ!" He was shouting as loudly as his father did, but in absolute panic. I did the only thing he left me the option for; I blasted a stream of fire at the large dark cloud that hid the Queen. I kept it burning until the last wisps of purple vanished from sight. Fearfully I closed my mouth and looked.

The Queen stirred. I breathed a sigh of relief.

"No, Mamma! Bad Mamma!" Zeeim was squealing his displeasure.

"It's okay, Zeeim," I said, breathing heavily. "She's alright. Look." Dibbins had taken her by the hand and pulled her slowly to her feet. She looked confused and dizzy—she was clinging to Dibbins in what I could see was an effort to stay upright. But she was very definitely alive, unhurt by the fire that had consumed her. Dibbins kissed her forehead, and I heard him tell her quietly that she could go and rest safely now.

Queen Hazebbul fainted.

"Dibbins?" I asked. "How did that work? At all?"

"From what I understand," he said, still breathing heavily, "Dragons have natural magic in them—"

"Duh—" I cut in.

"They also have an innate ability to undo the magic of others. Dragon fire is a particularly potent substance; it obliterates curses and such. Sometimes."

"Sometimes?" I asked. "So I might have just turned your future bride to ash?"

Dibbins looked at me, embarrassed.

[*Fig. 9, Dibbins and Hazebbul]*

I considered all of this as I flew everyone back to the palace. I felt sure that someone should have told me about dragon fire earlier in life; it was potentially very useful information.

Finally, we arrived at the palace. Dibbins instructed me to land in the front of the building this time. When I touched down, all of the guards tensed, their hands on their weapons, but no one moved. Then one, who was clearly a good deal brighter than the others, recognized Dibbins.

"Hail, Prince Arrik!" He shouted. All of the guards bowed, even though many looked disturbed by the image of the prince of the enemies carrying the unconscious form of the Queen into the palace. Nevertheless, they stepped aside.

The guards barred the door against me.

I harrumphed to myself, muttering about the rudeness of humans, and settled down onto the palace lawn. I had intended to sleep, but the combination of the excitement of the previous night and the stares of the guards erased that from the options list. Finally, in frustration, I waved to the nearest one to come to me.

"Y-yes?" he stammered.

"Why are you all staring at me? I thought that was rude in everyone's culture except unicorns." The guard swallowed and glanced around uncomfortably. I felt something ridiculous coming on. "What is it?" I allowed a tiny bit of flame to spill out of me when I said it, causing the guard to jump back.

"W-we were just w-wondering-ing why you h-haven't eaten that-that-that rabbit." I chuckled.

"Listen," I told him, trying to sound reasonable, "dragons mostly eat rocks. I don't even *like* meat. And if I did, I certainly wouldn't eat a creature who has Language. I don't know where all the stupid rumors come from. Dragons are not barbarians; in fact, we've had a civilized society longer than you have." The guards looked dubious; in a moment of brilliance, I called out in Human for Zeeim to come sit by me. His response was perfect.

"But Mamma, I'm *eating!*" I smiled and said,

"Alright, go ahead and finish." The guards all looked astonished. "I am hungry, though. Tell me, what does your kingdom have to offer in the way of stones?"

When Dibbins came back outside a full half hour later, I was surrounded by a hill of rocks in flavors I'd never tried before. Zeeim was sprawled on the grass next to me, snoozing, and the guards—who were actually not bad once they stopped being afraid—were watching me eat in fascination. I was describing Spendidium to them when Dibbins interrupted.

"Iz, the queen wants to speak with you when she wakes up."

"Alright," I said, "what about?"

"No idea." He flopped down onto the lawn. "But I think it's time for my breakfast too." A guard, catching his meaning, scurried off toward what I assumed was the kitchen. Dibbins looked around.

"Why is it that when Carobbin is at war with Lethina, the people in the palace are so helpful to me?" I assumed the question was rhetorical and ignored it, but one of the guards responded.

"Begging your pardon, your highness, but this war doesn't sit right with any of us. That's why we offered to guard the palace instead of going out to fight. And, if you'll excuse me, you have long loved the queen and would have been our king years ago if luck had run better with us. We suspected that the war wasn't really her idea." Dibbins and I glanced at each other. I shrugged, and he turned back to the guard.

"It's true. Well reasoned, soldier," he said. If I had been the guard I would have been seriously annoyed by the lack of information, but he just nodded sharply and turned back to his post, looking satisfied.

Dibbins, Zeeim, and I sat out on the lawn until evening, eating when we were hungry and chatting with the guards and each other. Zeeim was especially popular, and got four of the off-duty soldiers to play hide-and-seek with him. The guard who had explained the allegiance of the soldiers to Dibbins sat down on the grass with Dibbins and me, discussing the state of the war with us.

"It seems like the soldiers get some kind of craziness in them," he said. "I've seen them when they've just come back from the front lines, and they're not like normal soldiers newly off duty. They're obsessed with killing the enemy and capturing Lethina. It's strange. It takes them weeks to return to normal sometimes." Dibbins and I glanced at one another.

"Sounds like more magic," I said.

"Yeah, it does. I'll have to ask the Duke of Magic about it when I get home." Dibbins shook his head. "In'zdul is clearly a powerful sorcerer. Otherwise he couldn't have fought back against the spell from last night from so far away. I'm afraid of what else he can do." I didn't know what to say, so I just watched Zeeim as he sneaked behind a shrub.

"Dragon Izznae and Prince Arrik of Lethina," called a high, stringy voice; I turned my head and saw a man carrying a scroll and shouting from the palace steps. "Queen Hazebbul of Carobinn bids you enter her palace and speak with her." The scroll man snapped his paper shut, turned on his heel, and marched inside. He oozed an ego that made me want to set him on fire; I have a cousin like that.

"Well," I said to Dibbins, "time to go stop this war once and for all, I guess," I gathered up Zeeim, nodded to the guards in farewell, and marched into the palace.

I realized as I walked that I liked everything in Carobinn better than in Lethina. Where the palace walls of Dibbins' home had been a pristine white and the floor was made of some ultra-shiny wood, Queen Hazebbul's palace walls were painted in warm, cheerful colors and the floors didn't look like they would shatter if I touched them. Plus the halls were wider. The tapestries hung periodically on the walls of Lethina had depicted battles and slaughter; here, they showed healings, moments of great diplomacy, and beautiful landscapes. *Go Carobinn,* I thought, *I'm rooting for* their *jousting team.*

Scroll man strolled pompously in front of us, leading the way, until Dibbins (who seemed as annoyed with him as I was) sent him away, informing him that he—Dibbins (okay, he referred to himself as Prince Arrik)—knew the palace as well as anyone. Scroll man bounced away, looking deeply offended. Good. Dibbins did know where to go, it turned out, and we knocked on the door of the Queen's reception hall only a few minutes later. Queen Hazebbul herself answered it, ushering us in with a tired smile.

Dibbins lounged on a couch as the Queen settled herself onto a chair. I sat on the floor, and Zeeim sat next to me. I laughed to myself when he tried to wrap his tiny krane—his tail—around himself; the poor rabbit was going to grow up thinking he was a dragon. But I decided that was an issue for another time and focused on the Queen.

She was different than I had expected. While she was unconscious, she seemed very weak to me; even when she was speaking to Dibbins around the enchantment, it had seemed like the ravings of a worn-down slightly crazy person. Now as I looked at her I saw that, despite her exhaustion, she was every inch a queen. She sat up much straighter than any dragon could (in our defense, we have curved spines.) More than that, power seemed to radiate from her in a halo. For the first time, I respected a human on sight. This woman was not one to be mocked. I bowed my head.

"Dragon Izznae," she said, and my head jerked back up, "I thank you for the great service that you have already done for me and for my country, for my betrothed, and for all of the people of Lethina. Perhaps all of the people of Daiines." I nodded awkwardly.

"Of course, your majesty. Sure thing." I said. *Sure thing?* I thought disdainfully. *Sure thing? Wow, that was awful. Grow a jeed* (I believe humans say, "grow a spine"), *Izznae. You're a dragon.* I sat up taller, filling the room.

"I have a favor to ask of you now, though," the Queen said.

"What is it?" I asked. Dragons generally don't make promises before they know what they are agreeing to do. Queen Hazebbul turned to Dibbins rather than answer.

"Arrik, I believe you were right about the political situation. My soldiers will not receive orders for days, by which time they will already have broken into Lethina Capital."

"You can't use a magic mirror or something?" I interjected. Dibbins and the Queen both looked at me.

"The nearest magic mirror is in Lethina. The Carobinns certainly won't accept orders passed that way." Dibbins said. I snorted; humans are dumb sometimes. They should have a better way of communicating fast: if dragons need to hurry, we communicate through a pool of our own magical spit. It seemed like humans should've come up with something like that.

"So what do you want me to do?" I asked the Queen.

"I wondered," she asked, "how you would feel about carrying me to the front lines to speak to my soldiers myself."

Of course I said yes. Authority like the queen's is overwhelming, even for a dragon. We loaded up fast, much faster than I had expected. I refused to make the flight without getting some sleep first, but after my nap it was only about an hour before we were launching into the sky.

"You've been travelling like this for weeks, Arrik?" The Queen demanded. She had quickly gained a love for flying.

"It's been, what is it Iz, twelve days?" He asked. I

shrugged. He was right, of course, but I didn't want to think

about how long I'd been away from my family. They were not

going to be happy with me for leaving.

It was evening when we reached what appeared to be the

line of battle. The soldiers were wandering around in camps,

strolling in and out of tents. Hazebbul ordered me to the largest

camp.

I landed in the middle of a meadow which the soldiers

had clearly been crossing to reach the stream nearby. Hazebbul

and Dibbins stayed on my back as I meandered over to the

actual camp. When I arrived, as Hazebbul had said she

expected, a surprisingly young man was standing out to meet us.

"Queen Hazebbul," he said, dropping to his knees, "are

we riding dragons into battle now?" I had a feeling that this man

would be difficult to intimidate. "And I see that you've captured

the Lethinan prince. Wonderful. I am very impressed, your

Majesty." He stood again, staring hungrily at Dibbins. I suspected that if he could have breathed fire, Dibbins would have become a pile of ash.

"Wrong on both counts I'm afraid, general Miggdon," the Queen said in an icy tone. She climbed off of my back—with a bit of difficulty, but she kept her head above her feet—and stood to face him. "I'm here to declare an end to the war, effective immediately."

General Miggdon stared at her for a moment, then lifted his horn from where it hung at his side. He blew it twice, and soldiers began pouring out of the tents. They gathered in a large circle around us.

"Dibbins," I muttered in Dracogin, "this looks bad."

"It does," he said in the same language.

"Men!" The general shouted. "*Queen Hazebbul* has come riding a dragon—something she has never been heard to do before—to tell us that the war is at an end. What do you say to that?" The soldiers retained their stiffness from before—they were far too stiff, in fact, it looked unnatural—but a murmuring spread through them like a disease. A man about the age of Miggdon stepped forward, out of the circle.

"Sir," he shouted, "we will not end this war until Lethina has been captured, sir!" The murmur among the ranks of men changed to one that sounded approving. The man who had spoken stepped back as the general turned to him.

"Correct, Bythynn. Well said. Tell me, men," the general said, addressing all of the Carobinn soldiers again, "what shall we do about this order?" The muttering gained an angry sound.

"Imposter!" Shouted one of the soldiers in the crowd.

"What do we do with imposters?" Screamed general Miggdon.

"Kill her!" The shout came from all sides, and they began to march forward with the same unnatural exactness exhibited in their stillness.

"Iz!" Dibbins yelled over the soldiers, but I was already in motion. I whipped my krane around toward the Queen, knocking down four soldiers by accident.

"Hazebbul!" Dibbins shouted as I called, "Your Majesty!" The Queen looked around behind her and saw the escape. Grasping one of my aughts, she jumped onto my krane (not the most comfortable, but that was not the point, either.)

I roared out fire, sending soldiers diving for their lives in front of me. I ran through the gap they left and shot off into the air, leaving a crowd of Carobinns shouting insults and war cries behind.

CHAPTER TEN

Hazebbul was barely restraining her tears by the time we landed in Lethina Capital soon after our escape. Dibbins lifted her down off my back and led her by the hand into the palace. I followed at a respectful distance, wishing I had something to do. Just as Hazebbul's tears spilled over, Zeeim gave me an excuse to leave by demanding to see his female friend. By the time I had dropped Zeeim off in the royal warren and found my way back to Dibbins and Hazebbul, the Queen had regained her composure. They were waiting patiently for me to arrive.

"What now?" I asked them.

"Now we take counsel with my father," Dibbins said, "and then we stop this war."

"Dibbins," I said, "I like the way you plan. One step at a time is the best way to go." Hazebbul arched her eyebrows, but didn't argue with my philosophy. Which is a shame, really, because I love to make my ridiculous opinions sound reasonable.

King Roberr and the Duke of Magic arrived almost immediately after Dibbins sent word for them to come. We were back in the great dining hall. When the King entered he stopped and stared at Queen Hazebbul. Glancing at her, I saw that she had begun to cry a bit again.

"King Roberr," she said, and for the first time since the enchantment lifted she sounded like a child instead of a Queen, "I am so sorry for the trouble I have caused you. I am sorry for your people, for your land, for your fears, for your belief that I broke faith with you and with your son." King Roberr considered her for a moment, the look of masked emotion on his face. Then, mutely, he crossed the room to where Hazebbul stood and squeezed her like a child. He kissed her forehead and said loudly,

"I forgive you, my dear. I believe you were not acting as yourself?"

"No, but my country still owes a debt to yours—"

"NONSENSE." The King said. "IN'ZDUL OWES US A DEBT. The only thing you are guilty of is falling prey to a magic that could have ensnared any of us. You are still and ever will be like a daughter to me." The King peeked over at his son. "AND I STILL HAVE HOPE THAT YOU WILL BECOME MY TRUE DAUGHTER-IN-LAW VERY SOON." Hazebbul beamed, looking like she might explode from the emotions inside her.

"You mean you will still allow me to marry Arrik? After declaring war on your people?" Dibbins reached out and grasped her hand.

"WELL, IF YOU BOTH STILL WANT TO BE MARRIED, I SAY IT SHOULD HAPPEN AS SOON AS YOUR TROOPS WITHDRAW!"

"That might be a problem," I mumbled. Unfortunately the King heard me.

"DRAGON IZZNAE? WHAT DO YOU MEAN? THE CAROBINN TROOPS HAVE NOT RETURNED TO THEIR HOMELAND?"

Dibbins was the person, in the end, who managed to explain the situation to his father. As Dibbins spoke, the King's face grew more and more enraged and the Duke of Magic's face grew more and more petrified. When Dibbins finished explaining, the Duke interjected before anyone else could speak.

"This is bad news, my Lord, very bad," he said to the King.

"I noticed, Arrchann."

"No, you don't understand. In'zdul is using more than one branch of Kiteweyn. Think about it, your majesty. What are the five Great laws that must not be broken, set down by the creator of the gods?

"'Do not change any creature from being what I meant it to be; not in intelligence, nor in wisdom, nor in capacity, nor in stature, nor in gifts that I have given or not given,'" Hazebbul interrupted. "That's the first."

"The second is about respect for the dead," Dibbins said. "'Grant the souls of the dead their final rest. Do not bring them back from where they journey onto. Do not bind their souls to this world.'"

"I learned these too," I said, "Dragons sing them every year as we commemorate the gods and the first god. 'You are forbidden from forcing the heart of any creature to love or to hate, for they must choose for themselves.'"

"'OBEY AND RESPECT THE GODS WHO I GIVE UNTO YOU TO RULE YOU,'" said the King. "WHICH IS WHERE MOST OF OUR OTHER LAWS COME FROM, IF YOU THINK ABOUT IT."

"That's true, Sire, but it is these five Great Laws that concern us now. The last, of course, is, 'You must teach the laws unto your children, that there may be peace in the land.' Sometimes I wonder if the evil people in the world have forgotten the laws, if they were ever taught correctly. But no matter. The second law that In'zdul has violated is the law against forcing the opinion or feelings of any person. Clearly that was done to you, your Majesty," the Duke said, bowing to Hazebbul. "Thankfully that is an enchantment that can be lifted."

"And he has done the same to all of my soldiers?" The Queen asked, outraged. "How? How did he even cast the spell on me?"

The Duke, Arrchann, sighed.

"To place such a spell on you would have required him to touch you," he said. The Queen winced as if Arrchann had just told her she was infected with Blanderdans (it's a disease.

Don't you know anything about Daiines? It's awful and incurable.)

"How? If he had to touch me, how did he do it? Do you mean that he is inside Carobinn? Inside the capital? Inside the palace?" I heard the fear in her voice even though it wasn't visible on her face.

"Does Carobinn still continue the practice of allowing peasants to beg help from the queen?" Hazebbul's back straightened even more than normal, and she looked offended.

"Of course it does. Every week. I am as good a ruler as my ancestors!"

"I believe that, your majesty," the Duke said quickly, to stem her building frustration. "I was not questioning your ability to rule justly. What I meant is that In'zdul is a powerful sorcerer. I have no doubt that he could disguise himself as a peasant who came begging. And if he did, would it be so difficult to get the Queen to allow him to kiss her royal hand?"

Hazebbul had relaxed a bit when she realized that Arrchann was not questioning her capacity or right to rule. Now she slumped a little, looking despondent.

"Not at all. I brought this ruin on myself, didn't I?" Fast enough that it startled all of us, Dibbins took hold of Hazebbul's shoulders and turned her to face him. He looked at her tenderly (remember how much I hate emotional moments? This one was pretty high up in the annoying list) and put a hand gently on her face.

"Haze," he said, "don't blame yourself. It is not your fault that a wicked and conniving sorcerer took advantage of your good heart. Don't let this turn you to stone; your people love you because you are an honest and just ruler. Don't allow this one evil dwarf to destroy that. It would do damage to your kingdom beyond that of a thousand wars if they lost their trust in their queen." Hazebbul swallowed and nodded slowly.

"I'm sorry, Arrik," she said, reaching up to hold the hand that laid on her cheek, "I'm sorry to be so weak. I'm just so…afraid."

As Hazebbul spoke I realized that I wanted desperately to be friends with her. I knew somehow that she would understand the rejection I had faced from my peers, the loneliness of those years before Mooninga came, and even the loneliness after. It seemed that she was as reluctant to admit to fear as I was. I bumped her shoulder with my snout.

"This is a time when it is alright to be afraid," I said. "As long as you don't allow that fear to consume you. If it is a driving force for you, it may inspire you to do great things in the name of Carobinn." Hazebbul had turned around to listen to me, and when I finished she reached her arms around my neck and hugged me.

That was my first hug.

"Thank you, Dragon Izznae," she said.

"Call me Iz. We can be friends," I said. Hazebbul smiled and nodded.

"Wow, Iz," Dibbins said in Dracogin. "Somebody's grown up during our adventure."

"Oh, shut up," I said, "one of us had to and you certainly aren't." Dibbins and I both laughed while the Duke and the Queen stared. The King, who had understood the language we used, ignored the conversation and yanked us back into the present.

"SO HAZEBBUL'S ENCHANTMENT MAKES SENSE," he said, "BUT WHAT ABOUT THE SOLDIERS? DIDN'T YOU SAY YOU THOUGHT THEY WERE ALSO UNDER SOME KIND OF SPELL?"

"Yes," said the Duke, "not one that is as strong, but one that is harder to break entirely. Some soldiers with a strong will may abandon the war, but the spell will hang like a curse unless its power is completely broken."

"What is the spell in the first place?" Hazebbul asked.

The Duke thought for a moment, then explained,

"The best way I can think to describe it is that it's a huge cloud. Or perhaps it's a mist. It spreads through all of the people in its sphere of influence, affecting a thought here, a feeling there, until hatred and fury become natural and love and kindness become strange. It's not so much that your soldiers are enchanted to hate Lethina, my lady, but that they are enchanted to hate and Lethina got in the way of their rage."

"So how do we demolish the spell? How do I free my soldiers?"

"Well," the Duke sighed, "I would guess in this case that the old standby for getting rid of magic would be best. Since I doubt In'zdul has bothered to tie the spell to anything permanent—it would be a terrible misuse of his energy at this point—it's probably still attached to his person."

"So," I said, "if I were to roast him…"

"Or if I were to stab him…" Dibbins said,

"Or generally if we were to kill him," Hazebbul added,

"the spell would die with him?" The Duke nodded.

"Awesome." I said.

In'zdul was going *down.*

CHAPTER ELEVEN

Now, it's true that the gods have laws against killing. Let's face it, killing is just bad. But not as bad as the things In'zdul was doing. So I didn't feel too terrible about the idea of biting In'zdul's head off. Literally.

"Don't," Dibbins said when I expressed this thought to him, "I told you. He'd probably taste terrible. Besides, I thought you said dragons don't eat meat?"

"No, that's true," I admitted, "we don't. At least, not usually. But I never said I wanted to *eat* his head. Just chomp it off." Dibbins snickered.

"Well, you'll have a pretty tough time beating Haze to it," he said. I tried to think of a good comeback, but Dibbins was right.

"Zeeim is refusing to come," Hazebbul said behind me; I turned in surprise.

"When did you get here?" I demanded.

"In time to agree with what Arrik said last; I have the first shot at In'zdul. It's my country he risked."

"And, you know, mine," Dibbins said, reaching out and clasping her hand briefly. They were totally gross, they liked to touch each other way too much. I was considering forbidding them from holding hands on the trip to In'zdul's mountain.

"Um, and the free people of the world," I said.

"Oh, like that's not cheesy," Dibbins said. "You should put that on a poster somewhere, Iz."

"What, 'Free People of the World: come hunt dwarves with us, it's fun to watch their brains go smush'? Not likely."

"Eww," Hazebbul put in. "Let's avoid smushed brains. That's disgusting."

"So no Zeeim?" I said, changing the subject (it really is gross, you have to admit.) "While I hate to have him witness any more carnage, wouldn't he be useful? Maybe I can talk to him." There was a small cough behind me.

"Um, dragon Izznae, there may not be need for any carnage, as you put it." Dibbins, Hazebbul, and I turned to see the Archann, the Duke of Magic, standing in the doorway, holding a wooden box.

"What?" Dibbins asked.

"This is a jatkin," the Duke said. I stepped back instinctively.

"Where did you get that thing?" I roared, as Dibbins and Hazebbul said at once,

"A *what*?"

"It's a box that—" the Duke began.

"Destroys the lives of magical creatures everywhere, leaving empty shells and broken souls!" I snarled. I don't like to admit to fear, but I'll be honest, this thing scared the fire out of me.

"Iz?" Dibbins asked. "You okay?"

"NO!" I roared, spewing flame. The Duke jumped away.

"I would never dream of using such a thing against you, dragon Izznae," he said apologetically.

"What is it?" Hazebbul demanded.

"This box will drain the magic out of the intended target," the Duke said hurriedly. "In this case, In'zdul. Direct the open box toward him, say his name clearly, and it should take away all of his magic."

"I'll be honest, I don't want him powerless, I want him dead," Hazebbul said. "Maybe that makes me heartless, I don't care. He's evil. He deserves to die."

"Well, taking his magic from him should kill him," the Duke said. "It's keeping him alive, it has been for more than three hundred years."

"I thought the gods were keeping him alive," Dibbins said in confusion.

"No, my liege. The sacrifices In'zdul performs entice the darker pantheon of gods to ignore his heresy. His magic is what ties him to life. Powerless, he is also lifeless." The Duke smiled slightly.

"Thank you, Duke," Hazebbul said. "This is a marvelous gift."

"Don't thank me," the Duke said. "Thank the dragon Izznae. The jatkin came from her share of the stolen treasure." Dibbins chortled. I jabbed him in the chest with my krane and he stumbled back a bit.

"Ow!" Dibbins said, rubbing the spot where I'd hit him.

"You should have thicker skin," I told him.

"Settle down, you two," Hazebbul said. "Are we ready to go?" I looked around. The massive barn we stood in was the first building I'd seen in Lethina that wasn't made with perfect right angles and too-clean colors. There was hay and dirt and who knows what else strewn across the floor. It was comfortable; I would be sad to leave it.

"As soon as I convince Zeeim to come," I said, "I think we're all packed, and it's almost evening. We'd better get moving."

Zeeim, as it turned out, was only concerned that he'd be in the way. When I told him that we needed his help navigating our way to get In'zdul, he agreed to join us. Two people and a rabbit was a lot to carry, it's true, but not much more than two people without a rabbit.

As I flew toward Coortain, In'zdul's mountain, I thought over my adventure. The last time I'd flown to this mountain it was with a nasty little human on my back to steal some shinies and start my life. I hadn't cared about anybody or anything except my family and my treasures. Dibbins was right, I had grown up since then.

"Iz, can we move any faster?" Dibbins called out.

"Do you want to get off and push?" I hollered back, swishing my krane so that he rocked back and forth.

Okay, so I'd only grown up a little bit. Who wants to be totally grown up anyway? How *boring*.

"We've got trouble," Hazebbul called out as we approached the mountain. I'd been focusing on the peak, but I glanced now at the base of the mountain. It was ringed by lights which, after a moment, I realized were dwarves holding torches. Zeeim, perched on my head, began to shudder.

"Fire scorch them," I grumbled. "Now they know we're here." We had planned to land on the top of the mountain and attack at dawn. While the peak of the mountain was still the most easily defensible position, I'd hoped we could surprise the dwarves.

"What do we do now?" I asked.

"Land on top of the mountain anyway, just as we planned," Dibbins said. I circled the crest once, then landed.

"You realize they're all going to come charging up here to attack us, right?" I asked Dibbins.

"Probably," Dibbins remarked, "but look at the sky. It will be dawn soon. I hope they do come charging up here to attack us; the sun is their worst nightmare. If they get caught in it, they'll do anything to get us to let them go. Even lead us to In'zdul." I smiled.

"That is the best plan I've ever heard from you, Dibbins," I said. Haze kissed his cheek.

"Iz is right, Arrik, that is brilliant," she said.

Gag.

We set about making ourselves easy to find. Dibbins pulled an axe out of his eternally deep bag (now emptied of treasure) and felled a small tree. He chopped it into pieces and I set it ablaze. Then we sat down, Dibbins and Hazebbul melting cheese over the fire and smearing it across wedges of bread to eat, and waited.

It didn't take long. Zeeim soon pointed out flickering lights as they appeared between the trees, vanishing behind the foliage and reappearing seconds later a few feet closer. I stretched, moaning slightly.

"Looks like we have a pest problem, Dibbins," I yawned. His sword clanged as it slid out of the sheath.

"Well, we can't let vermin get close to the lady," he said. "Let's go take care of it."

"Be careful," Hazebbul said. I was about to tell her that the dwarves didn't pose much of a threat outside of their mountain, but she continued, "don't kill them all, or we won't have anyone to show us to In'zdul."

"I don't plan to actually kill any of them," Dibbins said. "Just to knock them out until the sun comes up, and that only if they neglect to give us the help we need." I looked up, scanning the sky. There were no clouds; the dwarves' reaction to sunlight in this weather would be quick and intense—blindness was certain, and it seemed likely that their clayish skin would heat, dry, crack, and bleed rapidly. After that, they would be in too much pain to move, and the problem would just get worse—leaving them out in the sun on a day like the one dawning would be a death sentence. They'd have to help us.

"We won't have to wait long," I said. "The stars have all disappeared already."

There was a rustling to the south and Dibbins raised his sword, scrambling to the southern side of our little clearing.

"Sk'annzde, put out your torch," someone whispered. I snorted. I'd give them a torch. I roared a roll of flame toward the whisper; there was a scream as a tree caught fire. Dibbins jumped forward. I heard a thud, another screech, and a *donnng* as the flat side of Dibbins' sword made contact with what was probably the dwarf's head.

"Dibbins, do you have something we can put out that fire with?" I called out lazily.

"I thought you could do that," Dibbins shouted back.

"Hmm. True," I said. I knocked the burning tree over, into the clearing, then sat on it section by section until the fire had been smothered. "Finished," I said as his head appeared from behind a tree a few feet to my left. He strolled out the rest of the way, dragging two unconscious dwarves behind him.

"The rest of them ran away," he said. "Cowards."

"Well, when have dwarves been known for their outstanding character?" Hazebbul said.

"Not fair," Dibbins said, "I've known some fine dwarves in my time."

"Fine, though, not outstanding," I commented.

"Fair enough," Dibbins conceded. "What do we do now?"

"Wait for sunrise and eat some more bread," Hazebbul said reasonably. I left the two of them to their bread, curling my krane around a tree and taking a nap. You know, a nap just before dawn. Whatever. I was exhausted; flying all night is hard work. When I woke up, Dibbins was saying my name.

"Iz! You have got to be the heaviest sleeper I have ever met!"

"Next time, you fly all night without a break. I'll doze on *your* back." I replied.

"Stop grumbling and hold down this dwarf, will you?" Next thing I knew Dibbins had forced a frantic, squirming, hairy little person between my snopps. I growled a bit and he stopped squirming.

"Please, let me go, the sun is coming up!" He shouted in terror (and in Human.)

"Shh," I said. "I detest loud noises." He looked up into my face; I smiled, showing my gleaming knoppers. He swallowed and stopped screaming, although he started twitching violently.

"You don't have to stay out here," Dibbins was saying to the other dwarf—a fellow with a dark, curly beard and hair to match. My dwarf was a green-haired and -bearded fellow with a globular nose.

"What—what do you mean?" Grunted Curly.

"Tell us how to find In'zdul. We'll get you underground."

"We value our lives," Curly snorted.

"Well then," Hazebbul said in a gentle tone, "I suppose we will have to keep you here with us." She stretched idly. "Mm, Arrik, have you ever stood on top of a mountain at high noon? You're so much nearer the sun, it's like it's twice as bright as usual. It's almost blinding. Glorious." She stared icily at Curly; even I got chills. She was good.

"He lives here, in Coortain," Bignose shouted from his place behind my fiings. He shuddered. "Under the mountain.

But you'll never get to him, his cave is the most secure place ever built out of dirt."

"Well," I said, flexing my fiings dangerously close to Bignose's neck, "Why don't you tell us what, exactly, makes it so safe for him?"

CHAPTER TWELVE

"Do you think they'll be alright down there?" Hazebbul asked as she climbed onto my krane.

"They're dwarves," Dibbins said. "They really like dirt. Weirdly a lot."

"They'll be fine," I said. It was true. I mean, it's not like the hole I'd dug for them was grand by any means, but they didn't have to sit directly on top of one another, and they were well hidden from the sun. "Ready?" I asked.

"Let's get going." Dibbins said. I took off. I barely bothered to flap my jeeds on the way down the mountain, I just fell artfully.

I landed on the opposite side of the mountain from where Dibbins and I had come the first time. There was a smooth sheet of stone that stretched almost higher than my head; Bignose and Curly had said that it was an enchanted door, one that only opened with a special password.

I knocked it down.

I glanced at the rubble as I stepped over it. It was thinner than I'd expected; apparently it was mostly for show. A sentry stood just inside the cave, cowering.

"Take us to In'zdul or my friend here will make a snack of you," Dibbins said from just below my head. I was startled; I hadn't realized he and Hazebbul had moved, but both of them were standing on the ground beside me. Zeeim was sitting on my head again.

The guard dwarf shuddered, but he looked Dibbins in the eye. It was almost impressive. But I was annoyed. So I picked the dwarf up in my knoppers and threw him out into the sunshine. Dwarves are tough; he wasn't hurt, but he immediately dug a hole in the ground with his bare hands and stuck his head in it.

Dwarves really, really hate the light.

"Zeeim, you'll have to look out for us again," I commented.

"Although it should be a bit easier: there are torches in this part of the mountain," Dibbins said. "Even dwarves use a little bit of light to get around." To prove his point, Dibbins rounded the corner and came back gripping a torch in each hand.

Dibbins and Hazebbul lead the way, while I whispered to them the directions Curly had given me.

"What in Daiines is 'puchink?'" Dibbins asked in frustration.

"Sorry, I forgot. Left. Turn left. I told you, dragons have a far more sensible system of giving directions than humans do."

The caves twisted on for about five minutes before we met the first armed guards. As planned, I roasted them. I didn't kill anybody, but they became interested very quickly in getting their armor off. And then, of course, Dibbins knocked them out.

I wasn't even sorry.

The next round of guards had a magician with them. I closed my eyes and held my breath so they couldn't enchant me again. I listened to the clanging of Dibbins taking on three dwarves and smiled to myself. It was a kind of music of its own. *Ahh.* I really was starting to get used to this adventuring business.

"You can open your eyes, Iz. They're all out." I peered into the semi-darkness. The dwarves were strewn across the ground. Dibbins stood, leaning on his sword and looking down at them. Hazebbul was fingering an axe that had apparently just changed owners.

"What?" She asked when she realized I was watching her. "I was trained in combat like any royal, and I was always good with an axe." I kept staring. "Breathe already, Iz, your scales are turning orange." I turned my head around as I exhaled, shooting fire down the tunnel behind us.

We continued like that for almost an hour, occasionally taking out some dwarves—Hazebbul turned out to be pretty good with her axe—before we came to another massive, smooth, shiny door.

Shiny.

Just pointing that out.

"Well, here goes," I said. Then I rammed into the door.

CHAPTER THIRTEEN

"Ow," I said as I bounced off the door. "That was supposed to come crashing down." I stared at the sheet of stone in stupefaction for a while before Dibbins put in,

"Maybe there's another way to get it open."

"Like what?" I asked. "Do you want to try ramming it? I think I sprained my ugdrugh..." (I did, by the way. The health-keeping dragon was not very pleased with me when I went to see him.)

"Perhaps all we need is a bit of magic," Hazebbul said.

"Probably," I said, "but I am not flying all the way back to Lethina to get someone who can help us now—especially not with my ugdrugh sprained!"

"Well of course not," Hazebbul said. "Now just hold on a minute." She reached into the pocket of her wide-legged pants—they looked like a dress from far away, but allowed her to straddle my krane for safer riding. I thought they were very sensible. If I were a queen on an adventure, I would wear pants like that. After all—

Fine. Then I won't share my opinion of human clothing. Your loss.

Interrupter.

Hazebbul searched in her pocket for a moment more, then pulled out a clumpy packet about the size of her fist. She unwrapped the cloth that had been wound around it, and pulled out what looked like a tiny version of the Duke of Magic.

It stretched.

It *was* a tiny version of the Duke of Magic.

My jaw dropped. (Don't pretend you weren't a little surprised too. I mean, who expects a queen to carry around a person in her pocket? Yeah, that's what I thought.)

Hazebbul set the minute Duke on the ground. The tiny man said something in a tiny voice; there was a blinding blue light, and the full-size Duke stood beside Hazebbul.

"Pardon me, dragon Izznae," the Duke said, bowing the Dibbins and me. "I thought this would be the safest way to travel. I didn't want to get chopped up if the dwarves were feeling axe-y."

"Why didn't you tell me?" I demanded as I pushed my jaw shut.

"I thought the look on your face would be priceless," Dibbins said. "So I persuaded Hazebbul to keep him a secret." He winked at his betrothed.

"Look, can you get this door open?" my newly closed jaw and I demanded, ending the formalities and the flirting. The Duke turned to inspect the door. He reached out, and a blue glow radiated from his palm. The light touched the door and the Duke jumped back.

"Vile magic, not to mention sloppy," he muttered to himself. "But mostly effective. Hmm. Interesting. I wonder if there is a way…" he trailed off, babbling his mumbo-jumbo to himself.

"This would be a really awkward time for soldiers to show up," I said. Dibbins nodded and stepped around me to block the passageway.

I yawned; Hazebbul noticed and spoke to me.

"What will you do when In'zdul is destroyed?" She asked.

"Well, I suppose I'll go home," I said. My family will be missing me—my parents will probably be furious with me for taking off. And I miss them too, especially Mooninga."

"Mooninga?"

"My little sister. Usually she and I are inseparable. Me being gone must have been hard for her. I wonder what she's been doing without me. It must be lonely."

"She has no other friends?" I didn't answer. "Well, you're a good sister, to take care of her like that," Hazebbul said. I felt the answer rising in me, even though I hated to give it.

"She's the good sister," I said.

"What do you mean?"

"Mooninga isn't lonely without me," I sighed. "She's popular. Other kids like her."

"Well of course she has other friends, everyone does—"

"No," I said. "Not me. Other dragons don't like me. Except for Mooninga, you and Dibbins are the only friends I've ever had." I sighed, only barely remembering to keep my flames in check. "Mooninga has probably barely missed me." Hazebbul put a hand on my forearm.

"Well Iz, *I* am going to miss you. And so will Arrik."

"Thanks, Hazebbul." I smiled.

"Um, excuse me, your majesty? Dragon Izznae?" The Duke had stopped muttering to himself and was looking at us in triumph.

"Did you figure it out, Arrchann?" Dibbins asked, popping up beside me. It was freaky how he kept doing that.

"Yes, my lord. I believe I did." The Duke was smiling so widely I thought his face might break in two. Dibbins, Hazebbul, and I waited, staring at him.

"Well?" I demanded. "How the blazes do we get in?"

"Normally it would be impossible," he said. "In'zdul has guarded his chambers against everything but the *poncux*, the five rarest substances in Daiines." The Duke continued smiling, as if this explained anything. I suppose in his mind it did.

"Pretend that none of us has studied magic our entire lives," Dibbins said with more patience than I would have. The Duke coughed quietly, embarrassed—whether for us or for himself I couldn't tell.

"Right. The poncux are five magical materials that humans consider almost impossible to gather. They are known for having healing properties, overcoming enchantments, and even granting luck. They were discovered in the first age; legend says that—"

"What *are* they?" I demanded, unable to endure his potentially long-winded speech any more. The Duke sighed.

"Water from the centaur's magical pool of Aet'uiran, the powder found in the secret compartment in unicorn hooves, the leaves of the IgG tree of the land of the giants, sand from the invisible beach on the southernmost coast of Daiines… and baked dragon tongue."

"What was that again?" I asked sharply. Actually, I asked so rapidly that it came out as, "whatwasthatagain?"

"Baked dragon tongue," the Duke repeated slowly.

"You are NOT baking my tongue. That's disgusting. And I need it. For eating and talking and sticking out at people and—"

"I wasn't planning to cut your tongue out. Relax," he said.

"Then what are you intending to do?"

"As your cells die and are replaced by newer, healthier ones, bits of flesh from your tongue remain awash in your spittle. Considering that you have breathed fire recently, these specks should be cooked enough to be magically effective. This is, understand, only a theory—I have never had experience with a dragon to test it—but it seems scientifically sound to me. If this is ineffectual, we will—"

"Think of something else," Dibbins interjected. "Did you get all of that, Iz?"

"Spit?" I asked.

"Spit."

"*Spit?*"

"Spit." The Duke nodded pompously.

"Spit, Iz," Dibbins said.

"I know, it's ridiculous, isn't it?"

"No, Iz, the dwarves are coming, a whole army of them! Spit! SPIT!"

I spat. All over the door. The shininess faded and I slammed into the slab of stone. It shattered, and the Duke, Hazebbul, Dibbins, and I dived in the room. The Duke made some kind of magic door behind us, sealing out the dwarf army. Then we all turned to face the room.

The very air seemed darker, and it seemed to be sucked toward the middle of the room. The room smelled like that nasty combination of dirty socks and bananas that I'd smelled when Dibbins and I removed the enchantment from Hazebbul. Standing quite serenely in the middle of the room was a dwarf in a mud-brown cloak, his faded, grey-streaked pink hair and beard combed with something greasy-looking. He looked old, like he should be falling apart just standing there, but a kind of filthy power oozed out of him nonetheless.

In'zdul.

"You're uglier than I thought you'd be," I said to him.

"Really?" Dibbins said. "I thought he'd be about this bad, maybe even worse."

"It's alright," Hazebbul put in. "He'll be an unoffensive pile of dust in a few minutes."

In'zdul laughed, a creaky, groaning laugh.

"You're better than the last group who tried to kill me," he said. His voice made me flinch. "They didn't make it this far. They tried to break down the door. It shredded them."

"Why didn't it shred me?" I asked. It was really more of a rhetorical question, but the Duke grunted an answer anyway.

"Dragon."

"Thanks," I said.

"Dragon." He said again. The word barely escaped his lips. I whirled to look at him; he, Dibbins, and Hazebbul were all being squeezed to death by enchanted chains.

"What do I do?" I roared.

"For them?" In'zdul said lazily. "Nothing. There's nothing you can do. You simply become my slave, like everyone else who crosses my path." I began to feel very tired as he spoke; I really hadn't had much rest lately.

"You rest here, in the dark, in peace."

"Dragon." The Duke managed. It was enough to wake me up a little. I was a dragon. I hated being underground; I hated the dark. I was a dragon. I was nobody's slave, and especially not to this tiny, hairy figure who was more wrinkled than anyone I'd ever seen. I was a dragon. He couldn't hurt me. But I could probably hurt him.

As soon as the thought occurred to me, another wave of fog rolled into my brain. I knew I was a dragon, and that I had a name—a good, draconic name, too, although I couldn't

remember precisely what it was. I knew there was something

important about the tiny fellow with the sparkly buttons, too, but

I couldn't remember what it was.

"Mamma, look, sparklies," Zeeim said, trying to be

helpful.

I didn't *mean* to attack. I just meant to pull that garment

with the sparkling buttons off of him. Unfortunately—or,

perhaps, luckily—dragon teeth are not made for removing

clothing.

I lunged my head forward, and bit In'zdul's head off.

He screamed, and a taste of salt and dirt and broccoli and

bad air washed through my mouth. He lost control of the spell—

naturally—and I remembered why I was, where I was, and who

I was. I spat his nasty head out; his body reached out and

reattached it crookedly to his shoulders, where it grew back in

place. I spat again, onto the ground, trying to get the awful taste out of my mouth. In'zdul was still screaming, but I didn't notice. I was looking down at the puddle I'd made. Dragon spit. The Duke had said it was known for several things, including healings—no wonder In'zdul's head had connected to his body, my slobber had helped it. But the Duke had also said that dragon spit could help end enchantments.

I turned and spat all over the chains holding Dibbins, Hazebbul, and the Duke. A shimmering orb in a sickly green color oozed above them, and my spit dribbled to the ground.

In'zdul chuckled behind me out of his now-crooked head.

"STOP THAT!" I screamed. I was too angry to think clearly; even though I knew it wouldn't kill him, that he could probably bind me up with magic again any moment, I turned toward In'zdul and blasted him with my hottest fire.

The flames curving away from him from some cursed magic made me realize what was missing. I scraped my teeth against my tongue, praying my last idea would work, and spat

all over my friends again. Then, in desperation, I flamed at the

foul bubble surrounding them. The chains strangling them

collapsed to the floor, mere iron. Dibbins, Hazebbul, and the

Duke gasped and choked, exhausted but alive.

"The poncux. Naturally. It doesn't matter, I can kill them

anyway," In'zdul said, watching curiously. "And once I own

you, I will remove your tongue, and you yourself will roast it for

me. And I shall use it to gain more power than ever before! You

will strengthen me a hundredfold, reptilian fool!"

"Right on one count," I grumbled. I am reptilian, but I

am certainly not a fool.

"In'zdul," Hazebbul whispered behind me, her voice

worn from being nearly strangled. In'zdul and I both turned to

look at her. She was still on the ground, shuddering, but she was

holding open the jatkin.

In'dul stared, and then all at once he started screaming. The light, which had seemed somehow dimmed by evil, faded, becoming a natural gold color from the torches. The stench of In'zdul's magic faded, replaced by a fresh, earthy, springtime scent. Then as suddenly as it had begun, the screaming stopped. There was a hush, and a pile of dust spread across the floor where In'zdul had stood. His cloak fluttered to the ground.

CHAPTER FOURTEEN

"Well." I said. I couldn't think of much else to say.

"Well done, Iz," Dibbins choked out, reaching up. I grabbed his forearm in my snop and pulled him to his feet.

"Well done Hazebbul," I said, helping her up. Then I lifted the Duke to his feet.

"And well done to you too, Duke." I said. "None of this would have worked without you.

"And we wouldn't have gotten here without you, Dibbins."

He grinned in a satisfied sort of way.

"Me?" Zeeim interjected.

"We'd have been in the bottom of a pit somewhere without you, little one," I added.

I thought getting out might be hard, but when we left In'zdul's cave, the entire dwarf army was sitting, feet together, heads down, trembling.

[Fig. 10, Army in the Halls]

"Fascinating," the Duke whispered—his voice had been completely worn out during the strangling. "It appears that they were under some kind of enchantment rather like Queen Hazebbul's soldiers. But they have born it for so long that they became dependent on In'zdul's magic."

"Rebuilding their kingdom will take time." Dibbins said, taking Hazebbul's hand.

"Yes," she moaned through her damaged throat, "and I know what you're thinking, and it's very nice of you, but we'd better get our kingdom settled before we can help out the dwarves of Coortain."

"*Our* kingdom?"

"I intend to have our wedding just as soon as we can both sing our vows." Hazebbul said. She coughed, then turned to face me. "And you will be my maid of honor. Won't you?"

"Hazebbul, you don't have to do that," I said, my scales blushing lavender.

"I know that perfectly well. But who better?" She leaned in and whispered,"I grew up pretty much alone too, Iz," she said. "I was different, just like you. It's nice having a friend around. I *want* you to be there."

I don't remember the march out of the caves very well. I was exhausted, and overwhelmed, and confused, and frightened, and excited, and it was all a little too much for me. I know we got out though, and that I took off for Lethina immediately. I wanted to get as far from Coortain as I could.

All three humans and Zeeim fell asleep on the flight home, and I collapsed on the floor of the royal barn almost as soon as we landed. A stable hand woke us in the morning. He shouted in surprise.

"Dibbins," I moaned, "can't you keep your servants under control? I detest being woken up before I'm ready." Dibbins laughed, then coughed.

"Riin, get my father, would you?" He asked. The stablehand grinned and nodded.

King Roberr shouted his pleasure at the top of his voice when Dibbins reported the news of In'zdul's death. Naturally.

I flew Hazebbul back to Carobinn as soon as I had rested. She demanded that her army return home immediately; they had already turned around before she gave the order. Once that was finished she flew into planning the wedding, although apparently she had it mostly planned already.

I knew I should have gone home, but I couldn't miss the wedding. Plus, I would probably be grounded for at least fifty years once my parents saw me.

"I think you're scared," Hazebbul said when I told her this. "I think you're a different person—or dragon I guess—than you were when you left. You don't know how you'll fit in now."

"Well, I can't fit in worse than I already did," I snorted.

"Don't snort, you'll set the linens on fire," Hazebbul said, almost managing to sound stern.

"Well, at least then you would choose which one you want to put on the tables!"

I liked having friends. It was fun.

The wedding was a ridiculous human affair, fabric everywhere and human nobles jumping at the sight of me. Which was pretty funny, I'll be honest.

Hazebbul and Dibbins were happy, though. Zeeim and his girlfriend wandered around with large bows tied around their necks, nibbling the grass. Naturally, the ceremony was outdoors where I could attend. That was nice.

I liked the ceremony. Dibbins and Hazebbul exchanged shining rings and sang a duet about their eternal faithfulness to each other. King Roberr wept—loudly, of course. The nobles in attendance looked happy, and I imagined most of them were; after all, Lethina and Carobinn would both have a more stable government now that Dibbins and Hazebbul were finally married. A few looked faintly jealous. Ah, well, that's to be expected.

I stayed until the afternoon after the wedding, lounging on the back lawn. That's where Dibbins found me.

"I'm glad you stuck around, Iz," he said. "I would have been awfully sorry if you had left before I got a chance to say goodbye."

"I wouldn't have done that," I said. "We've been through too much in the past weeks. I'm going to miss you, Dibbins."

"You don't have to leave, you know, Iz. You could stay here, work for the kingdom, we could fix up a barn for you in Carobinn…"

I sighed.

"In some ways I'd love that, Dibbins. But I can't stay, you know I can't. I have to go home, I have to see my family. I had a life before you showed up in my cave. I can't just choose a new one out of nowhere."

"I know," he said. He reached up, and I ducked my head down, and he hugged me.

"Can I join in?" Hazebbul had come outside. She threw her arms around me and Dibbins, squeezing us both tight.

"I have to give you your wedding present," I sniffed.

"Iz, there's no need, you saved both our nations," Hazebbul objected.

"Let me give you your gift," I said. "I know how hard it will be to fix the things that were destroyed in your little war, and even after that, Coortain will need help. So…" I stepped to the side, so they could see the grass that had been behind me. Piled there was my half of the treasure.

"Iz, no—" Dibbins started to say.

"I don't need it. You do. I would sit on it, and stare at it, and do nothing. You will use it to do good. So do some good with it. And remember me." I felt sick inside, giving up all that

treasure. *Stupid conscience.*

As Dibbins and Hazebbul walked away, hand in hand,

Zeeim and the chocolate-colored female—Punnhe—bounded up

to me.

"Are you leaving, Mamma?" Zeeim asked me. He had

grown up so much since that morning when I'd found him by

accident. Rabbits grow a lot faster than dragons.

"Yes, Zeeim. Are you coming with me?" He looked at

Punnhe. Then, sadly, he looked at me. I bent down so that we

were on eye level with each other.

[Fig. 11, Izznae and Zeeim]

"No, Mamma. I'm staying here, where there is grass. You live in a place of fire and stone. I—we—can't live there."

"No," I sighed, "you can't. I wish you the best, Zeeim. You and Punnhe both."

My first tear in years slid out as I flew home. I was leaving all of my friends for a lonely life. My heart weighed so much it was amazing I could even fly. I flapped my way over the edge of Spendidium.

"IZZNAE!" I heard a shout. Mooninga was flying toward me as fast as she could; she actually crashed into me in mid-flight. I hadn't expected to smile as I flew home, but I couldn't help it. My sister's laughter was contagious.

"What happened to you?" My mother asked as I landed in the home cave.

"I saved two countries and maybe the world."

"That's my little girl," my mother said.

"We're proud of you," my dad rumbled from behind her. Both of them nuzzled my head. Dragons aren't very good at hugging.

[Fig. 12, Dragons Trying to Hug]

"I have a surprise for you," Mooninga squealed.

"It's very sweet, she's been working so hard." My

mother said.

"Come on, let me show you!" Mooninga said. She led me outside and across the volcano. We landed in my little cave. Except... it wasn't my little cave the way I had left it. Gone was the hole Dibbins had dug on his way in. Mooninga had clawed and chewed out the cave, widening and deepening it until it was big enough for one dragon to live in. She had polished the sparkly walls and made holes in the ceiling to give them some light to reflect. She'd built a nest in a side chamber for me to sleep in and, most incredible of all, she had gathered a few treasures from neighbors so that I had the beginnings of my own hoard. Smiling, I added the now-useless jatkin—a gift from Dibbins and Hazebbul—to the pile.

"Do you like it?" Mooninga asked excitedly.

"I love it!" I exclaimed. "Mooninga, I can't believe you did this for me! How did you get Mother to agree to it?"

"I convinced her that you needed it. I didn't have to work very hard; she knew I was right. You grew up faster than most dragons, Izznae. You're ready for this."

"I'll miss living with you, though," I said.

"Well, that's why I added a second room and a second nest," she said, showing me a room hidden around the corner. "So I can come visit when I'm having teenage tantrums."

I smiled.

EPILOGUE

I woke with a start. A muffled scraping sound was coming from the back of my cave. Again. I edged out toward the sound. Dirt was flying up. I waited, slightly nervous. The scraping sound stopped.

"Rcz?" I heard.

"What?" I asked. The scraping sound came again. Then there was a lound bang, and a shout of frustration.

"Dibbins?" I called, hoping I wouldn't wake anyone up. I scooped the dirt away. There, in a hole just below my cave, stood Dibbins. Again. Covered in dirt. Again. I pulled him up into my cave.

"Thanks," he sighed, breathing heavily.

"I'm guessing your machine broke again?"

"Oh no," Dibbins said, "this one is new, a hundred and forty moving parts. Glorious."

"And broken," I laughed.

"For now," Dibbins said.

"Welcome to my cave," I told him. He sat down.

"Thanks. I'm glad you have your own place." I smiled; silence bubbled between us.

"Why are you here, Dibbins?"

"I have news. Hazebbul is going to have a baby!"

"A baby?" I gasped. "You should have started by telling me that!" Then I laughed. "You're behind. Zeeim and Punnhe have had two litters of six."

"You hear from Zeeim?"

"He sends me news every few weeks. He seems happy." There was a pause.

"We talked about it, Iz. We want you to be the godmother," Dibbins said. I stared at him.

"Me?"

"Who better?"

I smiled. It's true that the baby would be unimaginably safe; still, surely there was a downside? I considered. I liked babies. I missed having little Zeeim around, and a baby human would stay young longer. And I certainly wasn't ready to have draclets of my own!

"Okay, Dibbins. I'd love to be your baby's godmother." I hadn't come up with a single negative point.

"Wonderful! Haze will be thrilled. There is one thing, though."

"What's that?"

"The baby can hardly have a godmother he—or she—doesn't know." He turned toward the passageway. "We built a barn for you, Iz. Think it over." He disappeared down the hole.

"You're leaving already?" I called after him.

"I have to get home; I have a kingdom to run!" I stared after him.

"I could've given you a ride!" I called down the tunnel.

"Izznae, what's going on in here? You're going to wake the whole clan." Mooninga had flown across the lava.

"Dibbins was here. He wants me to be godmother to his baby!" Mooninga grinned.

"You'll be perfect for that. You're great with little ones."
 I laughed.

"A human child is a bit different than a draclet, Mooninga."

"And from a rabbit, too, but you managed that very well."

"Thanks." Silence filled the cave again, but it was comfortable, sisterly silence.

"Mooninga, you know there's not a lot for me here," I said. She frowned at me. "No, you know I love you, but you also know I have to live my own life."

"That's what the cave was for." She was sad, I could see it in her eyes.

"Would it break your heart, Mooninga? If I moved to Carobinn?"

My little sister studied my face.

"I think it would break your heart not to go, Izznae."

"What?"

"You'll always fit with me, you know that, but… maybe there's a bigger adventure out there for you than swimming around the lava pool. You grew a lot when you were gone, and it's like… it's like you're trying to get back into your egg. You're too big now. You're too extraordinary for Spendidium."

I smiled at her.

"It's not like I'd be all that far away. A day's flight, maybe. You could come visit. All the time."

I didn't have much to pack. Mother sent me with a diamond for Hazebbul; it's a traditional show of respect among dragons for new mothers. Father nuzzled my head and told me to be a good girl. And I flew off to Carobinn.

And that, my dear, interrupting reader, is the story you wanted to hear. That's the story of my first experience with humans. That's the tale of my adventure, and of my awesomeness.

Well, that's the beginning of it, anyway.

About the Author

Brynne Nelson is a wife and the mother of three beautiful girls. She has been writing stories since the age of seven. Her preferred genre is middle-grade fantasy, although she both reads and writes other things. This is her debut novel.

Made in the USA
Las Vegas, NV
09 May 2021